ARCADE

AND THE GOLDEN TRAVEL GUIDE

Also by Rashad Jennings

The IF in Life

THE COIN SLOT CHRONICLES SERIES

Book 1: Arcade and the Triple T Token

ARCADE

AND THE GOLDEN TRAVEL GUIDE

RASHAD JENNINGS

WITH JILL OSBORNE

ZONDERKIDZ

Arcade and the Golden Travel Guide
Copyright © 2019 by Rashad Jennings, LLC
Illustrations © 2019 by Rashad Jennings

Requests for information should be addressed to:
Zonderkidz, *3900 Sparks Dr. SE, Grand Rapids, Michigan 49546*

Library of Congress Cataloging-in-Publication Data

Names: Jennings, Rashad, 1985–author. | Osborne, Jill, 1961–author.
Title: Arcade and the golden travel guide / Rashad Jennings; with Jill Osborne.
Description: Grand Rapids, Michigan: Zonderkidz, [2019] | Series: The coin slot
    chronicles; 2 | Summary: In Virginia for the summer, Arcade and his friends
    restore a local mini golf course and continue to follow the token on fantastic
    adventures, in spite of recent troubling incidents. |
Identifiers: LCCN 2019010861 (print) | LCCN 2019014567 (ebook) | ISBN
    9780310767374 () | ISBN 9780310767435 (hardback)
Subjects: | CYAC: Adventure and adventurers—Fiction. | Miniature golf—Fiction.
    | Brothers and sisters—Fiction. | Friendship—Fiction. | Magic—Fiction.
Classification: LCC PZ7.1.J4554 (ebook) | LCC PZ7.1.J4554 Ap 2019 (print) | DDC
    [Fic]—dc23
LC record available at https://lccn.loc.gov/2019010861

Illustrated by: Alan Brown
Art direction: Cindy Davis
Interior design: Denise Froehlich

Printed in the United States of America

19 20 21 22 23 /LSC/ 10 9 8 7 6 5 4 3 2 1

To ALL kids and kids at heart . . .

I trust that by now you've enjoyed book one of The Coin Slot Chronicles—Arcade and The Triple T Token. If you haven't yet, there's still time to get caught up. Believe me, we're just getting started!

I'd like to dedicate this second book to you, the readers. You are blessing me with the incredible privilege of introducing the world to the undying kid in me—Arcade Livingston. I assure you the Arcade in me is alive, well, and still thirsting for wisdom, knowledge, and understanding. And I am absolutely honored to have all of you along for the journey!

I'd also like to give a shout out to my brothers Butch and Bryan, who always encourage me and challenge me to GO FOR IT!

And last, I pray that something you read in this— the second book of Arcade's incredible adventures—will help you in your own great quest to becoming the best version of yourself . . . Happy travels!

Going UP or DOWN?"

The voice blaring over the speaker in the elevator sounds a lot like . . . mine?

Zoe, my older sister who *begged* me not to use the token this time, crosses her arms and leans against the elevator wall.

"Arcade, you heard yourself. Are we going *up* or *down*?"

I throw my hands up and stomp a foot. "I don't know! I've never been given a choice before."

I feel for the gold chain around my neck. The Triple T Token is not hanging there now because I dropped it in the golden coin slot when glitter fell from the ceiling and elevator doors appeared in the living room of our brownstone.

Yeeeeah. It's been an unusual couple of months in New York City.

Loopy, my chocolate-colored Shih-poo, jumps up and scrapes on my leg.

"How did you get in here, Loopy?" I pick him up and

he licks my chin. He has gold and silver glitter stuck to his ears.

"UP or DOWN?" The voice on the speaker asks again.

"Um . . . Zoe, which is better, up or down?"

"Oh, so NOW you're asking me? No way, bro, I'm not gonna be the one to make the decision that dumps us in the middle of Siberia."

"Siberia? That would be cool! Cold, actually. I read about it in a book once." I pull Loopy in close and rub his neck with my chin.

Zoe rolls her eyes and plops down cross-legged on the elevator floor. "So what's your decision? Up? Or down?" She flings a hand in the direction of the doors. "All you have to do is push the right button."

I check out the elevator wall and my hands turn clammy. "ZOE!!! THERE'S ONLY ONE BUTTON!"

"WHAT?" Zoe jumps up and feels around on all the walls. "Only one button? That figures. The Triple T 'Transport to Trouble' *never* disappoints."

"That's not what the three Ts stand for."

"Then prove it." Zoe sticks out her index finger and pokes the air. "MAKE. A. DECISION."

I stare at the one red button and scratch my head. "This is confusing." Then, an idea hits and goosebumps pop out on my arms. "Hey, you think I could pick *sideways*?"

Zoe waves her arms wildly. "Who knows? There's only one button. Perhaps we could choose diagonal or circular . . . only it's an elevator, Arcade, and elevators only go UP or DOWN!"

"*We*? I thought you told *me* to decide."

Zoe sighs. "Leave it to you to think of something that's *not* one of the choices."

I shrug. "It's worth a try." I take a deep breath. "I choose . . . SIDEWAYS!" I reach out and push the red button.

Immediately, Zoe, Loopy, and I are thrown to the right side of the elevator as it speeds . . . SIDEWAYS!

"OOOF!" I slide down to the floor, holding Loopy tight. "I don't know where we're going, boy. So when these doors open . . . *if* these doors open . . . don't go running off. These adventures sometimes end in a—"

FLASH!

A bright gold flash fills the car. The elevator screeches to a halt. Zoe, Loopy, and I tumble to the other side and slam against the wall.

"OUCH!" Zoe lies in a heap on the floor.

I blink and wait for the white spots in my vision to clear, then push myself up. "I told ya sideways would work."

Zoe straightens her glasses and glares at me. "Looks like we've arrived in Siberia." She tightens the laces on her hot pink high tops and brushes glitter off her black leggings. "Too bad we didn't bring coats." She stands and waits for the doors to open.

DING!

CHAPTER 2

Home, Strange Home

The doors part, and we step out onto a parking lot across the road from rolling countryside. Dark clouds loom in the distance, but it's warm. No need for a coat.

Loopy jumps out of my arms and sniffs around near my feet. I look around at the homes dotting the hills, surrounded by acres of green grass and shade trees.

"Zoe, I think we're back in Forest!"

Forest, Virginia is where we lived until a couple months ago when we packed up our normal lives and moved to the craziness of the Upper West Side of New York City.

Zoe stares at the view and stretches her arms above her head. "Beauty and humidity. I *remember* this. Glad I'm dressed appropriately."

"Well, your fashion choices are a little rough." I laugh.

Zoe punches me in the shoulder and then steps behind me. She covers my eyes with her hands. "Turn around."

I do a quick one-eighty, dragging Zoe behind me, and she removes her hands. We're in the side parking lot of the old miniature golf course and arcade where my cousin,

Derek, and I used to hang out. But wait . . . did they repaint? Because the colors on the building look brighter.

"Forest Games and Golf." Zoe rubs her upper arms. "Much warmer than Siberia. Shall we go check it out . . . or would you rather go sideways?"

"Nah, I'm going *in*." I pick up Loopy and head for the side entrance. I've always liked playing in the arcade, even if it is a little run-down.

My jaw drops as we step in the door. The game room is packed! "Whoa, what happened to this place?"

It's a much different scene than the last time I was here. The games are all working! Ping-pong and air hockey tables are jammed with players. Big game consoles fill the room. And kids are lined up to play . . . pinball? The aroma of cardboard-crust pepperoni pizza hangs in the air, and people are even lined up for that!

Zoe reaches up and pulls her glasses off her face. She opens her eyes wide and puts one hand on her hip. "Something's . . . off."

I glance around at the crowd. "You got that right. These people's clothing choices are way worse than yours." I point to a guy in the pinball line. "Is he really wearing a denim hooded *vest*? It's so weird it's kinda cool."

Zoe grabs me by the arm and drags me out the front entrance. We both stand in awe of the mini-golf course.

"That windmill is fixed." I point to a windmill that's been lying on its side over the creek as long as I've been coming to the place.

Zoe shakes her head. "No, that windmill is *new*."

"Huh?"

"Hey! Kid with the red glasses!"

I put my hand up to adjust my red frames. Yep. He's talking to me.

An older, muscular guy with a little lighter skin than mine racewalks in my direction. He scowls. "Hey! No dogs allowed! Can't you read?"

"No dogs?" Oh, yeah, Loopy is still in my arms. He barks.

"Get him out of here. Now!"

The man points in the direction of the front entrance door where a sign about no dogs hangs. I hug Loopy closer to my chest. "I'm sorry, my dog just uh . . . followed me here."

The guy narrows his eyes at Loopy. "Dogs are a NUISANCE!" Then he steps back, his frown softening a bit. "I'll make a deal with you. If you pay for a round of golf, you can keep him this *once*. But only outside! And don't let him run around snapping at people's heels and stealing their golf balls!" Then he stomps off.

I look down at Loopy, who is panting, his tongue dripping saliva on the hot cement. "You hear that, Loop? Don't snap or steal."

"Do we really have to play a round of mini-golf?" Zoe wrings her hands. "The game stresses me out. You hit the ball in a hole up at the top of the hill and have no control where it comes out at the bottom. It always spits me out on the wrong side of a barrier."

I hand Loopy to Zoe. "Here. I'll go in and buy our games. Maybe my token will return and rescue you right in the middle of a bad shot."

The Triple T Token had been taking us on unpredictable adventures through the elevator doors since the old lady at the library gave it to me weeks ago. I still didn't know exactly how everything worked, but I *had* learned this: when the token heats up and glitter falls from the sky, it's best for everyone if I slip it in the golden coin slot right away. One time I didn't, and all my underwear burned up.

I pull open one of the double doors and jet over to the cashier line for the mini-golf games. Zoey's right, something's off with these people. The older teen boy in front of me in line is wearing a shiny green shirt with a HUGE collar. His date, a pretty girl who looks a little like Zoe but with *big* shoulder-length black hair, is wearing *two* pairs of socks—one scrunched on top of the other.

"Clubs and scorecards are over there." The cashier, a teenage girl wearing a purple blouse that makes her shoulders look puffy, directs the couple to the cart behind me.

They turn, hold hands, and give each other charming smiles.

Gross.

"You're going down, Dottie Jamison!" The boy is paying so much attention to his girlfriend that he bumps into me, causing me to drop my wallet.

He reaches down to pick it up. "Sorry about that, kid." He hands me the wallet and grabs the girl's hand again, walking her to the cart to pick out their golf clubs.

Dottie Jamison?

Dottie Jamison is my mom's maiden name!

CHAPTER 3

Golf Stalkers

My legs get all shaky as I step up to the cashier to pay for two rounds of mini-golf.

"Which course?" the girl with the really tall bangs and chunky jewelry asks as she chews half her gum. The other half sticks out the side of her mouth.

"Uh, which course are *they* playing?" I point to Dottie and her boyfriend, who are now walking out the double doors.

"Windmill course. That's a popular one. Might be a little bit of a wait at some of the holes."

"That's okay." I open my wallet to pull out some money. "How much?"

The girl shifts the gum to the other cheek. "Two-fifty a round. So five bucks."

I raise an eyebrow. "Really? That's cheap!"

She shrugs and chews. "Well, it's not REAL golf, you know."

I throw a five-dollar bill on the counter. "Clubs and scorecards over there?" I point a thumb over my right shoulder.

She winks. "You got it, genius."

I shove my wallet in my pocket, run for the clubs, balls, and scorecards, and take off to find Zoe.

She's right where I left her, holding Loopy. This time it's *my* turn to grab *her* by the arm and drag her. "Let's go. The course is getting crowded!"

She puts on the brakes. "Whoa, what's with all the mini-golf enthusiasm?"

I pull a little harder, but she just leans back.

"I have something important . . . to . . . show . . . you! Ugh, Zoe, why aren't you moving! You're so stubborn!"

She pulls her arm away and puts her hand to her chest. "Me, stubborn? You should talk, Mr. Sideways."

Ugggggggggh. Zoeeeeeeeeee.

I hold out a pink golf club to her. "Please. I want us to play behind a very interesting couple."

Zoe's eyes perk up. "Big collar and two pairs of socks? I saw them come out. They were so cute, and obviously in love. They couldn't take their eyes off each other."

"Yes, them!" I point over to the first hole of the windmill course, where the couple is getting ready to play. A family with five children has jumped in behind them.

I grab Loopy from Zoe and turn to walk toward the hole. Loopy jumps down and runs over to Dottie's boyfriend, who isn't wearing any socks, and starts licking his ankles.

"Aww, Abram, he likes you!" Dottie kneels down and scratches Loopy behind the ears.

My head breaks out in a sweat. Abram is my DAD'S NAME!

This adventure is getting real.

We wait while the couple take their first shots. Then they walk down the hill on the path, hand-in-hand.

"Sure, they're all happy now, but I bet one of their golf balls gets spit out behind a huge barrier." Zoe smiles.

"Zoe, their names are Dottie and Abram."

Zoe's smile goes flat. "What?"

"Yeah, I know. I think they're OUR PARENTS!"

"Whaaaaaat?" Zoe stares at me for a second, and then sits down on a bench and drums her fingers on her legs. The family of seven hits a bunch of terrible shots, golf balls flying all over the course so the kids have to chase them. One kid ends up in the creek.

"This is going to take forever." Zoe tightens her fists and walks up to the dad of the family. "Excuse me, sir, do you mind if my brother and I go in front of your family? We can skip this hole."

The dad wipes sweat from his forehead. "Please do. We could be on this hole for days."

"Thank you." Zoe returns to the bench and grabs her club. "Come on, Arcade." And she jogs down the hill toward the next hole.

Right before we get there, Zoe stops me. "If that's you-know-who, how are we going to keep them from recognizing us?"

I stop and put a hand up to my chin. "Well, let's think outside-the-elevator for a minute. If that's really you-know-who, and they're just teenagers, then they've never seen us because we haven't been born yet! Man, I don't get it, but this is *dope*!"

Zoe crosses her arms and drums her fingers. "So, Mr. Out-of-the-Elevator, do you think it's possible that they will sense future-kid vibes from us? I mean, we are *that* awesome." Then she points to my ankles. "And both you and Dad are not wearing any socks. That's DNA if I ever saw it."

I watch as Dottie pulls a hair tie out of her purse and pulls her hair into a ponytail, just like Zoe always does! Nerve sweats soak my T-shirt under my arms.

"Yeah, maybe we should keep a little distance." I reach down to see if the Triple T Token has returned yet.

Nope.

We hang back for a few minutes before we start the hole behind Dottie and Abram. Thankfully, the family behind us is still chasing balls up and down cliffs and into the parking lot. When we finally start our round on hole two, neither Zoe nor I can concentrate at all.

"I want to make *sure* it's them," Zoe says as she lines her

putter up with the ball. "I need to see their eyes up close."
She smacks her ball way too hard and it takes off like a
rocket. It lands right on the third hole green where Dottie
and Abram are playing!

"I'll be right back." Zoe's eyes are wide as she takes off
down the hill.

"Watch the vibes!" I shudder.

Loopy starts to take off after her, but I grab him. "Not
this time, boy. Sister's on her own." I duck behind a fake
bush and watch as Zoe approaches the couple. She says
something to them, and then points up the hill with her golf
club. Dottie and Abram look up in my direction and wave. I
poke my head out and wave back.

Then Zoe shakes both of their hands, transferring all her
future-kid vibes right into them!

ZOE!!! ARE YOU NUTS????

Her eyes are all bright as she trots back up the hill, and
she smiles bigger than I've seen in a while. "That's THEM!
That's MOM and DAD!" She has to take a deep breath and
sit on the bench with her head between her knees. "I think
I'm gonna faint."

I push her in the shoulder. "Don't faint! I wouldn't
know what to do about that while we're, well . . . here."

Zoe lifts her head. Her eyes are a little glazed. "Dad
looks just like you, Arcade, except he has that outdated
hairstyle. And Mom . . . I thought she would recognize me!
She asked me my name, and it just came out—Zoe. She
grinned and said she LOVED that name."

Thunder roars, and the black clouds we spotted earlier

have moved overhead and begin to open up on us. I put out my hand to catch some raindrops. "No glitter yet. I guess we get to stay around a little longer."

Zoe grabs Loopy and tries to shield him from the rain. "Run for cover!" She takes off toward the game building with all of the other soaked golfers.

I take off running too, but I slip on the slick ground and almost eat it on the concrete. Then lightning strikes the hill behind the course, and the rumble from the thunder practically knocks me off my feet.

"Hurry up, Arcade!" Zoe yells.

I glance up at the big sign in front of the place, and I'm frozen where I stand in the downpour. The sign no longer says Forest Games and Golf.

The sign says . . . Arcade Adventures!

CHAPTER 4

Triple T Transfer

Zoe! Come HERE!" I wave my arms and jump up and down until she comes back out in the rain.

"This better be worth my hair getting wet and frizzy." She grimaces and squeezes her ponytail, wringing the water out of it.

I point to the sign. Zoe sees it, and her jaw drops.

"Whoa."

"Yeah, I know."

"That's what it says on the back of your token."

"Yeah, I know."

"Do you suppose—"

". . . that this is where my token came from?"

We both nod and say, "Yes," at the same time.

Loopy barks. The poor little pooch is drenched like us.

"We gotta go find Mom and Dad!" I head for the building.

Zoe points to Loopy. "But that guy said to keep him outside."

I shrug. "In this weather? Come on."

The arcade is now more packed than before. Kids run around waving tickets they've won at the different games, and the pizza man cranks out slices of what actually looks to be decent pizza. I'm tempted to buy a piece, except that I want to follow my parents around some more. I hope they haven't dumped their golf equipment and already exited to the parking lot.

Zoe scans the room, her hand shading her eyes to keep off the glare of the neon lights flashing around. She turns her head left, then right, and then she stops. "I found them. Follow me."

We push our way through the crowd until we're a few feet behind them. They're standing in front of "The Claw"—that game where you use a handle to direct a huge claw above your favorite stuffed animal. You push the button, the claw opens and drops, and it usually grabs NOTHING, resulting in frustration!

Zoe and I inch a little closer. I zip Loopy up in the front of my hoodie, partly to dry him off, and partly to keep him out of sight.

My mom drops a few tokens in the machine. "I think *you* should try, Abram. I want you to get me that colorful cockatoo right in the middle." She points to a green and white stuffed bird that looks a lot like my sister's annoying bird, Milo.

No! Don't go for that! You'll be sorry!

"Are you sure you don't want to try it yourself?" Dad lifts mom's hand and places it on the handle.

She pulls it away. "Yes, I'm sure. I want you to win something for me."

I open my mouth and put a finger in to pretend to gag.

"Stop it, Arcade." Zoe puts her hands on her wet cheeks. "They're so cute I could cry."

Dad rubs his hands together, then pulls them apart and blows on them. "Okay, here we goooooo!" He grabs the handle and pulls it left. Then he bumps it right. He pulls it back. Mom puts her hand on his shoulder and bounces up and down on her toes. "You can do it. That little birdie is mine."

Dad pushes the button, and the claw opens, then drops. Zoe clenches her fists.

"Aw, come on, you wouldn't wish a stuffed cockatoo on them, would you?"

She gives me the stink-eye.

We look back toward the claw. It has closed, but not on the cockatoo. Dad's shoulders droop and he hangs his head. "I'm sorry, Dottie."

Mom hugs him. "That's okay. It means a lot that you tried."

And then the claw raises up. It is holding something—a little gold container, shaped like an egg at the top, but with a flat bottom. The claw moves over to the payoff chute and drops it down.

"Looks like I wasn't skunked after all." Dad reaches down and pulls the container out. "I wonder what's in here?" He holds the container over Mom's head and pretends to crack it.

Mom laughs and pulls it from his hands. "Hey, don't mess my hair up."

I shake my head. "She really *is* you, Zoe."

Zoe puts a finger to her lips. "Shhhhh!"

Mom holds the container for a minute and shakes it a little. "Hmmm. It feels special." She looks up at Dad and grins. "I'll treasure whatever it is, because you won it for me."

Enough with the love. Open it!

Mom pops the flat bottom off and gives it to Dad. Then she pours the contents out in her hand.

Zoe and I inch even closer. They don't notice us because they can't take their eyes off the prize. Mom hands the other piece of the gold container to Dad, and then she holds the prize up for him to see.

It's a golden chain. And at the end of the chain dangles a GOLDEN ARCADE TOKEN!

Zoe gasps and covers her mouth with both hands.

"It's beautiful," Mom says, raising up on her toes to give

Dad a kiss on the cheek. She hands it to him, and he lifts it up to examine it.

"Triple T, huh? All I've ever seen before on these tokens are double Ts."

Mom shrugs. "I told you, it must be something special."

Dad drapes it around Mom's neck. "So, do you like it as much as the cockatoo?"

She smiles. "A *hundred* times more."

And then the whole place breaks loose. Every game pumps up the music and the neon lights flicker brighter than before. Zoe and I wedge ourselves between a pinball machine and a wall across from the claw machine. Mom and Dad look all around and put their hands out as if they are wondering what has just happened. Glitter falls from the ceiling, on top of them.

Oh, man, I've seen this before!

The dog-hating guy who yelled at me earlier comes running toward Mom and Dad. "Kenwood! I found it! You put it in the claw machine, you rat!" He reaches his hands out toward Mom, and she steps back. Dad jumps in front of her to shield her from the big guy.

And then they both DISAPPEAR! Well, they could have just ducked through the crowd and slipped away somehow. But Zoe and I know better.

"THIEF! You little THIEF! That was MINE! GIVE it back!" The big guy is about to bust a vein in his neck.

"Let's get out of here." Zoe grabs my hood and pulls me from the hiding place. We scoot through the crowd, out the side exit, and back out into the rainstorm in the parking lot where we started.

I feel something heavy and cold drop on my chest, right over my heart. It's the token! We look up to the sky. The raindrops are now silver and gold glitter. Elevator doors appear, and so does the golden coin slot.

I pull the chain out from under my shirt and give the token a tug. It comes off the chain easily. I slip it into the slot.

"Get us outta here!" I yell, and I make an open-door motion with my hands.

The doors open, and Zoe, Loopy, and I scramble in.

or DOWN?"

hear my voice again over the loudspeaker. And, yes, still only one button.

nything but sideways." Zoe's eyes are glazed over.

ow just what to say. I reach over and press the

ne."

CHAPTER 5

Derek's in Trouble

The elevator delivered us back to our new home in New York City. It's part of a brownstone building, and we have really soft couches in the living room. Zoe and I plopped down on them, exhausted.

"Welcome back! Triple T! Bawwwwk!"

That was Milo, the *real* cockatoo.

"I wish *you* were in the claw machine," I called to him, only half kidding.

Then I heard whimpering coming from the other couch. Zoe was over there with her hands over her face, shaking.

I sat up. "Are you okay? Did you get hurt on the ride back?"

"No, I'm not hurt at all. I'm OVERWHELMED! Arcade, we just saw our mom and dad before they were married! And I think that big guy yelling THIEF was the same guy who wrestled you to the ground after the career expo today!"

As I was trying to process all that, my phone rang. It was my cousin Derek's special ring. "Oh, yeah! I forgot about Derek!"

Derek is my cousin and best friend who lives in Virginia. We're the same age and practically spent every moment of our lives together until I moved to New York. Derek's the nicest guy you'd ever want to meet, but right before Zoe and I traveled through the elevator doors, I had gotten several texts from Derek saying he was in some kind of trouble. I thought when the doors appeared that I was going to help him.

I put him on speaker. "Derek! Are you all right?"

I could hear a basketball bouncing in the background.

"Arcade! Finally! Things are getting intense around here! I think someone's after me, and it has something to do with you!"

"*Me*? How do you know that?"

"I was helping somebody and . . . I found somethin'. It was an accident. Oh, man. It's a long story. You gotta get out here!"

"Derek, where are you?"

"At the school gym. I'm afraid to leave. This big silver truck followed me here."

Zoe leaned over to talk to me. "Where's Aunt Weeda?"

"Hey, Doug, can Aunt Weeda pick you up?"

"Nah. She's workin'. She won't be home till tonight."

"How about Celeste? She could knock a few people out for ya."

"Arcade!" Zoe is always a little defensive when I talk like that about Derek's older sister, her best friend, Celeste.

"What? She's scary, Zoe, and you know it."

"She is NOT." Zoe grabbed the phone from my hand. "Derek, call Celeste. She'll know what to do."

I took the phone back. "And if she doesn't, call 9–1–1."

"Okay." Derek bounced the ball harder, faster. "Oh, hey, a couple of my friends just came in. Maybe we can walk out together. Arcade, you need to get out here so we can figure this out!"

I ran over to check the calendar hanging in the kitchen. May 9th. School would be out in a week. "Derek, you think you can hold out for a few days? I'm gonna see if my parents will fly us out for a couple of weeks."

"Yeah, man, I'll try to keep a low profile until then. I'm so glad you're comin'."

Zoe was now standing next to me, shaking her head. "And how are you going to talk Mom and Dad into that?"

"I don't know, but you're going to help me figure that out, right?"

She nibbled on her pinkie fingernail. "Sure. No problem at all."

"Derek, I'll see you in a week."

"You're the best, Arcade." The ball bounced three more times before he hung up.

That night, after dinner, I lay on the couch, exhausted.

It had been one of the craziest days ever . . . even *before* Zoe and I ended up in the sideways elevator to Virginia. We had just finished up a successful career expo at my school and were walking home, when my mom's stolen suitcase—I call it Daisy because of the daisies all over it—full of library books rolled out from behind some bushes. I ran for it, and a guy jumped on me, trying to rip the Triple T Token off my neck. Thankfully, I was rescued by my favorite police K-9, Samson, and his partner, Frank, who told Zoe and me to run straight home. Which is exactly what we did, but then those elevator doors—

The phone rang in our apartment, snapping me out of my daydream.

"Oh, hello." It was my mom's voice talking to someone on the other end. "Yes, we can do that . . . You too. Thank you so much, officer."

Officer? I sat up on the couch. *That can only be one person.*

Just then, my mom walked into the living room.

"Arcade, the officer from the 20th precinct asked me to bring you down to the station tomorrow morning to look at some pictures." She sat down next to me and put a reassuring arm around my shoulders. "I know it's been a tough day, but it would really help."

Tough? You have no idea, Mom.

Or did she?

Thankfully, the rest of the night was uneventful. The Triple T Token kept its cool. It would have been nice for it to transport me out of there the next morning, though, as I was having a tough time at the 20th precinct. It was tricky giving them information, without giving up *certain* information, if you know what I mean.

"Arcade, we'd like you to take a look at these photos and tell us which guy tackled you on the sidewalk."

Mom paced the room. "I can't believe this is happening. All over a silly suitcase full of books."

I scrolled through the photos on the tablet. It wasn't hard to pick him out. "This is him."

Officer Frank Langdon, the one filing the report, wrote down notes. "Yep, that's the guy we brought in. Sorry you had to come all the way down here to confirm. I'm glad Samson and I were at your career expo. Things could have turned out much worse." He turned to my mom and dad. "I'll just get this finished up, and then you can sign it. I'm sure you want to press charges."

"You bet!" Mom said. "No one comes after my kids and gets away with it."

We went out for a lunch of traditional New York style thin crust pizza, which was interrupted by a call to Dad. "Okay . . . yes. Thank you, Officer Langdon. We appreciate all that you've done." Then he hung up and gave Mom a funny look.

She stopped, the pizza slice in her hand halfway to her mouth. "What?"

"Lenwood Badger."

She dropped the pizza on her plate. "Lenwood?"

"That's an unusual name," Zoe said. "Like Arcade. Hey, are you ever going to tell us why you named him that?"

Mom put her hand out to place Zoe on hold. "Lenwood Badger. What a fitting name for a creep." She grabbed her napkin off her lap, balled it up, and threw it onto her uneaten pizza slice. "I don't like it, Abram."

"He's in custody, Dottie."

"I know, but how are we going to keep the kids safe this summer with our increased work schedule?"

"*Increased* work schedule?" This time my pizza slice dropped to my plate. "You already have busy schedules."

Dad reached over and put his hand on my shoulder. "They just called on your mom to teach a summer session at the college, and I have another stage to design in addition to running *Manhattan Doors*."

My mom is an adjunct professor at the local college,

and Dad builds sets for Broadway shows. I haven't been to a Broadway show yet, but I've heard that *Manhattan Doors* is getting rave reviews.

I sat back in disgust.

"We're just going to have to get creative," Dad said. "Maybe you can take Zoe with you to work, and I can take Arcade with me."

Mom shook her head. "I don't want him staying up that late every night."

"We can stay at home just fine," Zoe said. "I'm almost fifteen."

"OR . . ." Everyone turned and waited for me to finish my thought. "You *could* send us to Virginia to stay with Aunt Weeda!" The brilliance of it all gave me goosebumps.

"Weeda?" Mom chuckled. "She's never home. She just started her third job."

Zoe kicked in some support. "Then we could help her keep up the house, and we could spend some time with Celeste and Derek. I think it's a great idea."

Dad shrugged. "At least we know everyone in that neighborhood."

Mom retrieved her napkin ball and began to eat her pizza again. "Gotta pray about that. But it sounds like it could be a good solution. IF Weeda is up for it."

"Are you kidding?" Dad said. "She would love for our kids to visit! I'm sure she misses pinching Arcade's cheeks."

I put my hand up to my cheek. "Oh, yeah. I forgot about that." Aunt Weeda has been chasing me around since I was little, pinching my cheeks. It's embarrassing.

"I really miss Celeste." Zoe pushed out her lower lip, making the saddest puppy-dog face I'd ever seen.

Mom tilted her head. "I still have to pray about it, but if Weeda is willing, I think it's a good idea. At least for a couple of weeks. Until we feel better about this Lenwood character. Lenwood . . . where have I met a Lenwood before?"

I turned toward Dad just in time to see him raise his eyebrows at Mom.

I think he knew.

CHAPTER 7

Return to Forest

The trip to Virginia came together without me and Zoe having to cook up a plan. And, better yet, Doug Baker got to join us! Doug is my best friend in New York. He lives with his grandma, who hadn't been feeling well, but who lately seemed to be on the mend. So, on the last day of school, my parents asked Aunt Weeda if Doug could come too. Aunt Weeda said, "Send as many as you want." Mom and Dad booked Doug a ticket. And the very next day, we wheeled our carry-ons into the airport to board a plane to Lynchburg, Virginia, which is just a few miles from Forest.

The only frustration was that I didn't have room to take all the books I wanted with me.

"They have libraries in Virginia, you know." Zoe hefted her mermaid suitcase up on the conveyor to have it examined by security.

"Yeah, they have libraries in Virginia, you know." Doug plunked his suitcase up on the conveyor. He tends to repeat people. Kind of like Milo, the cockatoo.

I lifted up Daisy. We'd been through a lot together.

After thinking she'd been stolen forever, it felt good to have her with me on another adventure.

Mom handed me the small dog crate with Loopy in it. "Have fun. Be safe. Do whatever Weeda tells you to do." She bent over the security ropes and kissed me on the forehead.

"Mom! I'm almost twelve. No need to slobber on me in public."

She put her hand up to cover a smile. "Sorry. Can't help myself."

"Zoe," Dad said, "you keep Celeste under control."

"Celeste? Who's that?" Doug was pulling random items out of his pocket and throwing them in a plastic tub.

Zoe rolled her eyes. "She's not that bad."

I laughed out loud. "Yeah, right!"

Zoe took Loopy's crate from me and poked me in the side with her elbow. "You want to go, right? Then, hush up."

"Move away from the security line!" The TSA agent yelled at my parents. Then he gestured to me, Doug, and Zoe. "Come forward."

"Bye, kids!" Mom and Dad backed up and waved.

I waved back, and my stomach churned. We were leaving for a month. That's the longest I'd ever be away from my parents.

Or maybe I'd see them soon on another trip through the elevator doors. I reached down for the token as I walked through the security scanner.

And I set off the alarm.

"Step aside, young man." The gruff-looking agent directed me to a plastic mat next to the scanner.

Zoe looked back from her cleared position in front of me. "Arcade, what did you do?"

"Yeah, Arcade, what did you do?" Doug had made it through, too, and already grabbed his suitcase off the conveyor.

I held up my hands. "Nothing."

Zoe let out a big sigh. "We'll wait for you over there." She pointed to a bench where people were putting their shoes back on after being cleared.

"Anything in your pockets?" The agent swirled a wand around me.

I reached down and pulled them inside out.

Surprisingly, no.

"Take off your belt."

"I don't have a belt."

"Anything around your neck?"

"Ummm . . . yeah." I looked behind me.

Where's Mom and Dad?

They were still back there, staring at me.

I turned toward the agent. "I have this chain."

The agent walked over to the conveyor and grabbed a round plastic tub. "Drop it in here."

I pulled it off as fast as I could, hoping Mom and Dad wouldn't see. But when I did, the golden token caught a reflection that made it look like I had lit a match.

I dropped it in the container.

"Okay, let's do this thing again," the agent said, and I turned to go back through the scanner. This time there was no alarm.

I did catch Mom's eye. She traced a u-shape with her finger under her neck and grinned.

I flashed my toothiest smile and shrugged.

The young woman who was operating the scanning computer examined the token for a couple of minutes. "Are you hot? Cause this little piece of jewelry seems like it's glowing."

I fanned myself with my hand. "I'm a preteen boy. We're all hot."

She giggled and let the token through. "Happy travels."

I hurried over to the container, grabbed the chain, and quickly dropped it around my neck. If Mom saw, she didn't let on, because she just smiled and waved, looking a lot less concerned now that I made it through security.

The poor container though. The plastic had melted and there was a little round indentation where the token had been.

CHAPTER 8

Seeds

A isle or window?" Zoe shoved her carry-on into the overhead compartment, and then stood there, waiting for me to answer.

"Is that a trick question?" I stuffed Daisy next to Zoe's mermaids.

"I don't ask trick questions. That only leads to ridiculous answers. Like zooming sideways in an elevator."

"Okay, then, I'll take the window."

"Good. I like the aisle."

I stepped past Zoe and scrunched my way over to the window seat. At least a real captain was flying *this* plane— not like the last one I was in when we traveled through the elevator doors and my friend Scratchy was at the controls.

Or was someone else controlling that plane? Who knows with this Triple T Token around my neck.

I shoved my black backpack with the pink flamingos under the seat in front of me, secured my seat belt, and felt for the Triple T Token. I pulled it out of my shirt to examine it. On the front, there were three raised Ts, connected together. And on the back, in curved letters on the top and bottom, it said *Arcade Adventures*.

"Zoe, why do you think they changed the name of that old arcade from Arcade Adventures to Forest Games and Golf?"

Zoe pulled a flavored sparkling water from her backpack and twisted the cap off. "I don't know. It's been Forest Games and Golf as long as I can remember."

"And what do you think that mean guy at the arcade meant when he called Kenwood a rat? And who *is* Kenwood?"

Zoe chugged her water and stifled a burp. "You're giving me acid reflux, Arcade. How is it that you ask sooo many questions but you never seem to have good answers?"

"HEY, ARCADE! Check it out! I'm in the very back row!" I craned my neck to look back at Doug, who unfortunately got one of the last tickets on the plane, so he had to sit in front of the bathroom. "Signal me if you have to go! I'll save you a place in line!"

"Well, that's handy." Zoe laughed. "Can't wait to see how Celeste deals with Doug."

"Yeah, I'm a little nervous about that myself. He could end up with a mouth full of dirt."

"That was a long time ago. She's chilling out lately."

Celeste is the toughest girl I know. She can climb any tree she sees, she was on the wrestling team in junior high and beat most of the boys, and she teases everyone mercilessly—everyone except Zoe. One time, she chased a school bully home and told him she wanted to be his friend and she had a piece of candy for him. He just needed to close his eyes and open his mouth. The big guy was dumb enough to do it, and Celeste tossed in a handful of dirt.

"I wonder if Celeste knows anything about the people who are after Derek?" I shivered, thinking that we'd be in his neighborhood in a few short hours to find out what I had to do with all the trouble he was in.

Again, Zoe took a swig of water. "I have no answers for you, bro. Like I said before, maybe you should ask your token for advice."

It'd be great if the Triple T Token had come with an owner's manual. I reached down for my backpack, pulled out a green spiral notebook, and began to jot down everything I could remember that had happened to me since that old lady at the library draped the token around my neck and said, "Happy travels."

I . . .

. . . was thrown from a bull.

. . . operated on and saved the life of a K-9 German Shepherd.

. . . rescued Doug from a disastrous appearance on a food network.

. . . visited Yankee Stadium and got advice from the Babe.

. . . worked on a NASCAR pit crew.

I got so engrossed with my writing that I hardly remember the plane taking off. I scribbled away.

. . . ended up on a plane full of kids flying high over New York City.

That last adventure freaked me out more than any of the other ones! What if the token hadn't returned? What if Scratchy would've had to land the plane? I jotted more thoughts. Questions, actually. Pages of them. When I finally raised my head, a flight attendant was staring at me.

"Pretzels or cookies?"

"Huh?" I took off my glasses, rubbed the fog off them, and squinted at the lady.

"Pretzels or cookies?" She held out two snack-sized bags so I could see them.

Hmmm. I'm not feeling either one.

"Can I have sunflower seeds?"

Zoe choked on either a pretzel or a cookie. "Oh, puh-leeeeeze! Arcade, the choice is pretzels or cookies! Do you think the airline can cater to the whim of every person on the plane? Just pick one or the other."

I looked up at the flight attendant, who was trying not to laugh.

"Does that mean you don't have seeds?"

"Let me see what I can do." She turned and walked back to first class. She was back in an instant, with a little bag of sunflower seeds. "Here's a cup you can spit the shells into. Enjoy the flight." Then she pushed the cart to the back of the plane.

I popped a few seeds in my mouth. "Mmmm. Bacon ranch! My favorite!"

I'm glad I asked.

Zoe just glared.

"Aren't those pretzels a little dry?" I held the bag of seeds out. "Want some bacon ranch?"

"Why do you always do that?"

"Do what?"

"Ask for things that aren't on the menu?"

"*Everyone* knows there are things on the menu they don't tell you about."

"Uggggh! I'm going to talk to Doug."

Doug had an empty seat next to him. Zoe sat in it.

Fine with me. I got stuff to read.

I shoved my journal in my pack and pulled out one of my library books: *Shaping the Pyramids and Other Engineering Marvels.* I had checked the book out to help some of my friends find jobs to research for our sixth-grade, end-of-year career expo. Engineering didn't really fit me, but I renewed the book anyway because I knew there was something special about pyramids that I still needed to discover. Like something on the menu that I wasn't seeing yet.

I cracked the book open to the middle, where all the pictures were. There was an envelope with a note in it.

Dear Arcade,
Praying for your adventures in Virginia.
Remember:

> Guard your heart above all else, for it
> determines the course of your life.
>
> PROVERBS 4:23 (NLT)

I'm proud of you.

Love, Dad

My heart determines the course of my life?

Funny, it seemed like, lately at least, the token was doing that for me.

Doug plopped down next to me while I was pondering that deep thought.

"Man, you can't even recline your seat back there 'cause of the dumb lavatory! You want some candy?" Doug held out an apple sucker.

"Nah, thanks. It'll clash with my seeds."

Doug's eyes got wide. "It'll clash with your seeds? How'd you get *seeds*?"

"I asked."

"You asked? Did Zoe ask for somethin' and not get it? 'Cause she's awful mad."

"She's not *mad*. She just doesn't get me sometimes and that drives her crazy."

"'Cause you two are opposites?"

I looked over at Doug. "Yeah, I guess you could say that. We *are* opposites. And she drives *me* crazy too."

"I wish I had a sister. I wouldn't care if she was opposite me. It'd be nice to have someone to argue with."

I reclined my seat. "Do you and your grandma ever argue?"

Doug sat up. "Are you kiddin'? Who in the world would argue with their *grandma*? Nah, she's a saint. Plus, I've been real worried about her lately. She might have to move into an assisted-living place."

"Why?"

"She's been getting sick a lot, Arcade."

That sent a jolt through me. "Then where would you live, Doug?"

"Don't have a clue."

Silence.

Doug popped the apple sucker into his mouth and chewed on it a minute. Then he pulled it out and examined the sticky mess. "I guess I'll cross that bridge when I come to it. At least that's what Gram always tells me. Can I have some of your seeds?"

I held out the bag. "Sure."

I'm glad you asked.

CHAPTER 9

Visors Up!

The flight from New York wasn't long, but I was glad to escape the silver tube and get on solid ground with my sister, Doug, Loopy, and the token, all in one piece. As soon as we exited the terminal, I spotted Derek's bright yellow visor. He wears it upside-down, but forward on his head. He's already tall, and the visor adds even more height.

"Arcaaaaaade!" Derek ran over and gave me a fist bump, a high-five, *and* a chest bump. "It's about time you got here!"

"Dude, your visor!" I pulled it off his head. "That's not keeping a low profile."

Derek looked around the baggage claim area. "It's okay. I just put it on when I got here."

A hug session complete with squealing was going on between Aunt Weeda,

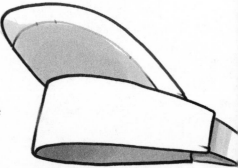

Celeste, and Zoe. Doug stood there watching them, like it was a train wreck or something. "They're kinda scary," he whispered to me behind his hand.

Celeste broke away from the hugs and approached Doug with a hand on her hip. Her short black hair was pushed up in a faded red ball cap, and she was madly chomping on her gum. Though she's Zoe's age, 14, she only came up to Doug's chin. She tilted her head to look up at him.

Here it comes. Celeste's first Doug insult.

She smiled. "Hello. You must be Doug." She held out a hand. "I'm Celeste. Welcome to Virginia."

What?

Doug cleared his throat and stood up a little straighter. "Thank you."

Then Celeste came over my way and whispered, "Hey, Arcade. Is every boy in New York as good looking as your friend?"

Oh, no . . .

I choked on my saliva.

Aunt Weeda bounded over, both her hands holding bags of snacks, just like I remember her.

"Arcade! I've missed you sooooo much! You want a snack?" She gave me one of the bags, and then she pinched my cheek. I jumped back.

"Gotcha! I'm sorry, baby, I just couldn't resist. I won't do it ever again. Look at you! You're almost a grown man."

A grown man? Hardly. But there was that time when I went through the doors and was a Doctor of Veterinary Medicine. And I had one hairy set of arms!

Zoe and Celeste came over to join us. "Mama, can we go out to eat somewhere?" Celeste scrolled through nearby restaurants on her phone.

Doug licked his lips. "I like eating!"

Aunt Weeda checked her watch. "Can't do it today. I have to be at work in forty-five minutes. But I tell you what, let's call the Bridgeview Bakery and pick up some chicken pot pies and a cake to celebrate! You kids can eat at home and share all the adventures you've had over the last couple of months."

Adventures, for sure. But how much should I share?

CHAPTER 10

Bridge View

erek, Zoe, and I ran into Bridgeview Bakery to pick up the food. Doug stayed with Celeste and Aunt Weeda. He had no choice, really. He was stuck in the back of the minivan. Celeste was talking his ear off, and he was repeating everything she said back to her.

"I love this place!" I stopped in the bakery parking lot to take a whiff. "We gotta get some of that cinnamon swirl bread too.'

"You got it, my man!" Derek held up Aunt Weeda's credit card. "I got the power right here."

Zoe opened the door. "I like the food, but I have a problem with the name."

"What's wrong with the name?" I stood there, filling my nostrils with cinnamon aroma.

"Bridgeview?" She put one hand on her hip. "You don't know?"

"Of course not."

Zoe pushed us back outside. "Take a look around. Do you see a *bridge* anywhere?"

We scanned the horizon.

Nuthin'.

"Now do you get what I'm saying? No bridge. No view. And yet it's the Bridgeview Bakery. *C'est ridicule!*"

When Zoe breaks out her French, it's game on. "Oh, wait!" I stepped up to within inches of her face. "I *do* see a bridge. It's the bridge of your nose. And I think there might be a zit brewing there."

Zoe pushed me back. "Haha. You know I have a point."

"You do. Again, I'm looking at it. Right at the end of your no—"

"DEREK!" A girl who looked about our age came out the door. "I saw the order for Weeda Clark. I hoped you would be coming for it."

The cute girl with the wide eyes and flowy black hair gestured toward the door. "Aren't you going to come in? Your order is ready."

We followed her in, and she bounced behind the counter and picked up a huge brown-handled grocery bag that had a picture of a bridge on it with the name of the bakery.

"Can we add some cinnamon bread to our order?" I asked, and I saw Zoe roll her eyes.

The girl's smile lit up her entire face. "Of course!"
Then she bounded over to the bread shelves and pulled out a
package of that sweet cinnamon stuff I'd been waiting for.

"How have you been, Arcade? I haven't seen you around
lately."

What? Who are you?

The badge she was wearing said her name was Jacey.
Hmmm. "I've been good. I moved to New York City a
couple of months ago."

Jacey put her elbows up on the bakery display case and
rested her chin in her hands. "Wow, New York City. Is it as
amazing as it looks in the movies?"

"What movies?"

"Practically every movie ever made," Zoe turned to
Jacey. "We haven't had a chance to visit many places yet."

Jacey sighed. "I'd love to go to New York."

Derek and I stood there like dorks, saying nothing. What
was I supposed to say? I didn't remember seeing her. Ever.

Derek waved Aunt Weeda's credit card. "So, my mom
gave me this. Can I use it, or does she have to come in?"

Jacey shrugged. "It's fine. I know your family, so
you're good."

Something suddenly hit me. "Are you *running* this
place?"

She giggled. "No, my mom's in the back, making more
pot pies. I like to help her in the summer." Then her left eye
closed and opened a couple of times. "Here you go." She
raised the food bag over the counter and handed it to me.
"Hope you enjoy the food."

"Oh, I will." I could practically taste the cinnamon bread already.

I turned, and my token sent a jolt of heat through my body. I stared at the large mural of a bridge painted on the wall opposite the bakery counter. It looked a little glittery around the edges. I wondered if anyone else noticed that.

"Jacey, what bridge is that?" I pointed to the mural.

Jacey smiled. "Mom says it's whatever bridge you need to cross."

"Oh. So everyone's bridge view might be different?" I glanced over at Zoe and smirked.

"Or the same. I know, I don't get it either. But I really like the mural." Her eye blinked again. "Arcade, if you need *anything* while you're here in Virginia, just call me here at the Bridgeview Bakery."

Now my cheeks heated up. "Gotcha."

And then I escaped out the door.

"She was friendly." Zoe elbowed me in the ribs. "What was her name again?"

"Jacey. Derek, do you remember a Jacey from anywhere?"

"Nope. What was wrong with her eye?"

"I don't know. Maybe she got cinnamon or sugar in it."

"Yeah, that's probably it. She was nice, though."

"Oh, she was *super* nice." Zoe grabbed the bag from me and headed for the van.

"Maybe we should put the Bridgeview Bakery number in our contacts." I pulled my phone out of my pocket.

"Yeah," Derek laughed. "You never know when we're gonna need some more cinnamon bread." We all took a minute and copied the number listed on the bag into our phones.

As we neared Aunt Weeda's gold minivan, Derek ducked down. He tipped his chin toward the street and whispered to me, "There it is, Arcade. That's the truck that's been following me."

I peered over at the silver truck with the tinted windows. It was parked in the road on the bakery side, but I couldn't see the driver. "Get in." I pushed Derek into the van and scooted in next to him in the second row.

Celeste and Doug were in a talk-fest in the back, and Zoe sat in front with Aunt Weeda.

Derek leaned over to me and talked real quiet. "It's been weird around here, Arcade. Ever since I helped that guy move, and I saw the post-it with your name on it in one of the boxes."

"You saw *my* name? Are you sure?"

"Yeah. How many Arcade Livingstons do you know?" Derek fished a green post-it note out of his pocket. "I've been carrying this around since the move. I feel like a thief since I took it out of his house."

I examined the post-it. It definitely said my name in bold printed letters. And right underneath it was a drawing of three Ts connected together.

"Who is this guy, Derek? Why did you help him move?"

Derek shrugged. "He's the guy who owns Forest Games and Golf. Remember him? Grouchy guy? We used to see him sometimes when we went to hang out there. I've been bored, so I went to play a game of mini-golf all by myself one day. He asked me if I wanted to make some money helping him move."

"Yeah, I know exactly who you're talking about. What's his name again??"

"He just told me to call him Mr. B."

CHAPTER II

Pot Pies and Pyramids

unt Weeda's living room is on the second floor overlooking the green front yard of 2300 Cimarron Road. It's filled up with one oversized couch. It's like twelve feet by twelve feet when you push all the ottomans together. There's no room for other furniture, but there's no need for it, because everyone fits on the couch together.

Zoe launched herself on it as soon as we walked in the door.

"Now this feels like home!" I let Loopy out of his crate and he jumped up on the couch too. Aunt Weeda doesn't care who's up there. Animals, kids, it's just one big happy couch family.

Aunt Weeda hurried into the kitchen and packed herself a lunch to take to work. She cut a sloppy slice out

of the pot pie and took a bite. "Mmmm! Bridgeview makes the best pies. Next to mine, of course." She set both pies out on the table. "Don't let this food get cold. Start eatin'! If you eat out on the couch, make sure you put it in my deep bowls so you don't slop it all over the place." Then she turned to Loopy. "I suppose you want somethin' too, right, Loop?" She pulled some dog treats out of the pantry and fed him one. "Boy, do I miss your family." She roughed up his neck. "But at least I have you all back for a month."

Aunt Weeda went to her room to get ready for work, and all us kids got out the deep bowls and spooned ourselves some chicken pot pie.

"This is crazy good," Doug said as he took a big bite and closed his eyes, chewing and swallowing in delight. "Did you all know that I'm going to be a food entrepreneur when I grow up? I'm going to have to check into the chicken pie business."

"Chicken pies are good." Zoe took a big bite and swallowed. "But I prefer sweet pies. Meat in pies just seems wrong. Plus, I like single crust pies, so I can see what's in them."

"Yeah, that figures," I said.

Celeste took a bite of her pie. "This *cannot* be wrong." Then she took her bowl out to the living room and sat in the middle of the couch. "Come tell us all about New York. How's city life? Whatcha got goin' over there besides cute guys?"

"Food! That's what's goin on. The food trucks are spectacular!" Doug plopped down next to Celeste.

The biggest thing Zoe and I had goin' on was the Triple T Token. But how were we supposed to tell our cousins about that? And now that I'd seen my mom and dad win the token at Arcade Adventures, there was *so much more* to tell them.

But I couldn't. Could I?

"School's okay." I grabbed a throw pillow and propped it behind my back on the couch. "But I was only at PS 23 for a few weeks. Now I have to go to junior high somewhere. We've got twin bullies, Casey and Kevin Tolley, who live across the street. I think they like me, but they'll never tell me that. Zoe goes to school with their older brother, Michael, at the high school for super-smart people. My favorite person in town is Ms. Weckles, the librarian at the public library."

"Sounds about right . . . for a book nerd." Celeste has been teasing me about how much I like reading for as long as I can remember.

"Call him a nerd if you want," Zoe said, "but readers are leaders. It's a fact."

"Yeah, I guess you're right." Celeste stared down into her bowl.

I tried to encourage her. "I didn't realize how many books there were about careers until we had to do that career expo project. What do you want to be when you grow up, Celeste?"

"That's easy. President. Or a drill sergeant. Some job where I can boss people around."

"She's been practicing on me my whole life." Derek had

put his visor back on his head and was looking much more relaxed since we drove away from the silver truck at the bakery. "I've been thinking about jobs lately. What if NBA point guard doesn't work out for me? I've been thinking about space a little. How did people figure out how to get up there? It's mind-blowing."

"Yeah, what do they eat in space? That freeze-dried ice-cream?" Doug scraped the last bit of pot pie from his bowl. "Who's ready for dessert?"

"Me!" I hopped off the couch to take my bowl to the sink, and I planned to grab a few slices of cinnamon bread.

The Triple T Token had a different plan.

"Arcade, what's wrong?" Zoe rushed over to me the moment she saw me fall on the floor.

I grabbed my chest. "I don't know. I mean, I do know. I'm just not ready. I haven't told anyon—" Sweat ran from my forehead into my eyes. "I hope Aunt Weeda won't mind a little glitter in the house."

Zoe reached out a hand to lift me to my feet. Doug, the only other one in the room who knew what the token could do, dropped his spoon and his eyes grew wide. "Oh, boy . . . where we goin' this time, man?"

"What are you talking about?" Celeste collected all our bowls and stacked them in the sink.

"Where's Loopy?" I pulled the token out from under my shirt. "We can't leave him here by himself."

"What's goin' on, Arcade? Why is your chest flashing?" The light from the token was shining on Derek's bright yellow visor.

Glitter began to fall from the ceiling.

"I guess we're doin' this!"

Elevator doors appeared, and so did the golden coin slot, pulsing light toward the token. All right there on top of Aunt Weeda's couch.

Celeste gasped.

"Duuuuuuuuude," was all Derek could say as he stood there in shock.

"Um, there's been some other things going on in New York that I probably should tell you about . . ." I wiped my forehead with the back of my hand, pulled the token off the chain, and placed it in the slot. ". . . but I don't have time to tell you about it right now."

Really? My mind raced. *Now? With all these people?*

Loopy must have heard the commotion because he ran in from the hallway. *Woof! Woof!* He jumped into my arms, panting, with his tail wagging.

"You like to travel, Loop?"

Woof!

"Okay then." I made an open-door motion with my hands, and the elevator doors parted. The room sparkled with gold glitter, and a sign displayed over the doors:

ALL ABOARD.

"Y'all comin'?" Sweat dripped down my back, and my whole body shivered with excitement. Or was it fear? The old lady at the library had wished me "happy travels" when she put the chain around my neck, so I was holding on to that hope every time I walked through the doors.

Celeste was the first to run in. "I don't know what this is, but I know I want to get out of Forest, Virginia!"

Doug was next. "Then get ready, 'cause you might even get out of this century!"

Zoe crossed her arms and walked in, shaking her head. "You guys don't know what you're talking about! I just hope the ride is a little smoother this time."

That left Derek. His body faced the elevator, but his eyes were looking out the living room window toward the front yard curb. "Hey, Arcade! There's the silver truck! He's watchin' us again!"

"Then get in!" Celeste ran out and pulled Derek by the ear. "We'll deal with it later."

With all of us covered in glitter and inside the elevator, the doors closed. My own voice blared over the loudspeaker:

"UP or DOWN?"

I hit my forehead with my palm. "Not again!"

"Not again!" Doug put his hand on my shoulder. "Not again, what?"

I stared at the unmarked red button. The only one. Again.

"I have to make a choice."

Celeste sighed. "It's not rocket science, Arcade. It's one or the other."

Zoe laughed. "You wish."

"How about we vote?" Derek said in a shaky voice.

"Nah, I gotta choose." I brushed glitter from my arms

and closed my eyes. I wanted to know more about my parents, and what happened after they won the token from the claw machine. Maybe we could go back there. If I just picked . . .

"BACK!" I yelled, as I pushed the button.

"HOLD ON!" Zoe screamed, and she squatted down on the floor in a ball.

The doors closed, and we shot . . . backward!

"AHHHHHHH!" Derek's visor flew off his head and tumbled around the elevator like it was in a clothes dryer. We all kinda did the same thing—first being thrown to the front and then rolling to the back when the elevator came to a halt.

"Get me out of here!" Celeste brushed herself off and moved to the front of the elevator. She touched the doors and pulled her hands back. "Whoa, they're hot."

Next thing I know, I'm sitting real high in the air, and a rock is sticking me in the behind.

"OUCH!" What in the worl—"

I'm sitting on top of a PYRAMID. I know, because I see other pyramids in the distance. Maybe I should have asked *where* in the world instead.

Egypt?

I'm by myself, and I'm scared. I expected to arrive with an elevator full of friends *and* my dog.

"Arcade?"

I turn in the direction of the voice, but instead of seeing my friends, I come face-to-face with the old lady from the library!

"Oh, hey." I haven't a clue what to say next.

Nice seeing you here . . . on top of a PYRAMID?

I don't have to say anything, because she speaks first.

"Are you enjoying your travels?"

"I would enjoy them more if I knew *where* I was going and *why.*"

The gold T on the ball cap she's wearing flashes light in my eyes. "That would take all the adventure out of it."

"You mean it would take all the fear out of it."

"Fear? There's no need to fear. Your travel guide knows where you're going."

"Travel guide?"

She points to my chain, which is missing the token on the end of it.

"You find out the *why* after you go. Traveling always teaches us something about ourselves. The people you meet. The adventures you experience."

"Who *are* you?" I scratch my head. "And why doesn't this pyramid have a pointy top?"

"Maybe you should ask the people who are building it."

She points toward the bottom of the pyramid. A crowd of people wearing flowing clothing and cloth draped over their heads are moving blocks of stone.

"Those are the *builders*? What year *is* this?"

"You chose *back*. You went back a little."

I stand and survey each side of the pyramid. "Whoa! How did they build this? It's a perfect triangle!"

"And if you look at it from above, it's made up of squares. Perspective is everything."

A jolt of excitement shoots through me. I *love* this kind of stuff! Wait till I tell Zo-

"ARCADE!" My sister's voice shakes me out of my thoughts. Her head pops up over the top of the pyramid— her hair dusty and matted from sweat. "Are you going to give me a hand?" She stretches her hand out, and I run over to grab it.

"Ugh." Her foot reaches the top of the pyramid and she pulls herself up. She brushes red dust off her knees and shades her eyes as she looks out at the horizon. "Are we seriously in Egypt?"

I nod. "Around 2500 BC. That's what my library books say, anyway. We're witnessing the building of the great pyramids! And did you know that a pyramid is made of squares?"

"No, it's NOT, Arcade. It's made of dirty rocks! That's what I just climbed. Dirt and rocks! I couldn't care less what shape. Why did you choose to go *back*? And where is everyone else?"

I turn to ask the old woman, but she's vanished. So inconvenient! I have hundreds more questions for her.

Loopy scrambles up one side of the pyramid. His chocolate-colored fur is now a dusty orange color.

"Loop! There you are, you silly dog!" I pick him up, and then I hear a scream.

"ARRRRCAAAAAAADE!" It's Doug. He's afraid of heights.

Zoe runs to the opposite side of the pyramid. "Arcade! We've got trouble!"

I rush over to where Zoe is. Doug is about a hundred feet down, his arms stretched over his head, his fingers clinging to a stone. His right foot is planted on a ledge, but his left foot . . . it's dangling, looking for a place to land.

"ARCCCCAAAAAADE! HELP!"

I set Loopy down, and I take off my sweatshirt. "He's gonna fall. I gotta go get him!"

Zoe digs her fingers into my shoulder to stop me. "Arcade, the stones are crumbly, you could slip and fall yourself!"

"But I can't leave him there alone."

"We're right under you, Doug! Don't panic!" I spot Celeste just below Doug's feet. And Derek is not that far behind her.

"I . . . can't . . . move!" Doug looks up at me. "I . . . can't . . . breathe!"

I lay on my belly on the top of the pyramid. "I'm going to go pull him up."

I begin to descend feet-first, and Zoe reaches her hand out to grab my shirt. "Arcade, be careful!"

It's hot, and my glasses start to slide down my nose. I let go of a stone to push them up, and my other hand slips! I tumble down a few feet, but I'm able to catch myself and plant my feet on a ledge.

Don't fall. Don't fall. Please, God, don't let me fall!

I take a minute to catch my breath, and then I ease myself down to where my foot is resting on the same stone as Doug's fingers. I pray I don't step on them.

"Arcade, I think I'm going to pass out."

"Hang on, Doug. Take a breath. You have friends above and below you. Try to take one step down."

"NO! I'm going to fall!"

"Would you rather step up, then?"

"Would I rather step up?"

"That's what I said."

"NO!"

By now, Celeste is on Doug's right, and Derek is on his left. They both grab him by his belt.

"You're safe, Doug. We gotcha." Celeste is smiling ear-to-ear.

"When I count to three," Derek says, "we're gonna push you, Doug. You just relax and place your feet on the stones as we go up."

I take a few steps up myself so I'm not in the way.

Doug whimpers, and his fingers slip a little. I pray again.

"One . . . two . . . three!" I pull myself up several feet, and Celeste and Derek heave Doug to the next stone.

Zoe watches with Loopy from above. "You got this, Doug!"

Derek calls out again. "One . . . two . . . three!" And this time they haul him a few more feet.

"I'm gonna die!" Doug's eyes look dazed and his arms shake. Clearly his fear has overtaken him.

"One . . . two . . . three!" Celeste and Derek heave, and Doug inches up some more. One more good lift and he'll be on top. But since the triangle is narrowing, Celeste and Derek have to push Doug up and wait to follow after him.

I pop myself on top of the pointless pyramid and turn to reach a hand out to Doug. "You got this! It's solid ground up here!"

Doug reaches and I grip his hand. I have to throw myself backward to drag him up.

He lies there on his stomach, kissing the crumbly rocks.

"H-h-h-ow are w-w-we going to g-g-g-et d-d-down?" Doug has tears forming in the corners of his eyes.

"I wish I knew."

It's all part of the adventure.

Celeste comes up the side of the pyramid next, followed by Derek and his yellow visor. "Great choice, dude! Looks like we're in ancient Egypt! Hey, where's the apex?"

"Apex?"

"Yeah!" Derek takes a look around. "You know, the pyramidion. The Benben stone. The top." Derek puts his fingers together to form a point.

Zoe laughs. "Derek, have you been studying pyramids?"

He shrugs. "A little. I'm intrigued by how they were built. It's math. Kind of."

"That's right, you like math!" When we were in fifth grade it was the only subject he didn't almost fail.

"It's better than any other subject, that's for sure. Uh-oh. Wait a minute." Derek takes a look over the side of the pyramid. "Whoa, baby! I think I see the Benben!"

"Where?" I walk over next to him.

"Down there, on the ramp at the bottom. In front of all those people. I think they're celebrating it coming up here!"

I watch as the Benben begins to move up the ramp, ropes pulling the massive stone inch by inch. It reflects the light of the sun, and it looks like solid gold! "But *we're* up here!"

Screams come from the people at the bottom of the pyramid.

"Arcade, they've spotted us." Derek backs up a few feet. "We better get down."

Zoe smacks her forehead with her palm. "Let's climb down the back."

"Back?" I pick Loopy up and hold on tight. "Which side is the back?"

"Arcade, stop it!!! This is *no* time for questions." She grabs my shirt and pulls. "*This* is the back!"

We make our way over to the edge. Ropes are hanging down that side, too, and people are pulling on them, staring up at us.

"Okay, nix that," Zoe says. "We're going down the side."

"But what about Doug?" I point to the lump of anxiety that is Doug, lying face down and holding onto the ground for dear life.

"We'll carry him." Celeste flips him over, sits him up, and drapes his arm around her shoulders.

I place Loopy up on my shoulders. "Hold on, boy, we're descending a pyramid in ancient Egypt. Who knows how it's all going to turn out?"

I turn and throw my feet over the edge, pushing my glasses up again. Man, I wish I could be on the other side to watch the apex, or whatever it's called, finally make it to the top of the pyramid. I drop down a step. "Are you guys gonna be okay with Doug?"

Celeste has pulled a bandana out of her pocket and is wrapping it around Doug's eyes. "Yep. Because he's not going to look. Right, Dougie?"

Dougie?

Despite what we're about to attempt to do, I have to stifle a laugh.

"Right, Celeste." Doug holds his shaky hands out. "Just get me down quick."

"And what do we do after that?" Zoe—always the planner. It's an annoying trait, even here in ancient Egypt.

"I . . . don't . . ." I look to the sky, and something coats my glasses so I can't see. I grab tightly to a stone with one hand so I can lift them off my face with the other. They're covered in silver and gold flakes.

Oh, yeah! Glitter to the rescue!

I drag myself back up to the top of the pyramid, where I see golden elevator doors in the shape of an apex. I feel a jolt of heat through my body as the token drops back on the chain.

"It's gold, Arcade!" Derek points to the apex.

I take in the view. The top of the pyramid really *is* gold. "That's DOPE!"

The coin slot appears in front of the doors, and I reach for the token to drop it in.

"Hey, Dougie! You might want to remove your blindfold for this."

"Hey, Celeste, I might want to remove my blindfold for this."

Celeste smiles and pulls the bandana off Doug's eyes. He rubs them a second before opening them. He pops up on his feet when he sees the doors and the coin slot. "SAVED! LET'S GET OUTTA HERE!"

I drop the coin in, make the parting motion with my hands, and we all rush in.

"UP or DOWN?"

I'm getting pretty tired of my voice giving me choices that I don't understand. But at least I know not to choose *back* this time.

"How about Weeda's?"

I push the red button.

CHAPTER 12

Sneaking Out

We landed back on Weeda's couch.

Oh, the softness.

Doug rubbed his eyes some more and stared at the ceiling. Then he turned on his side, grabbed Loopy, hugged him, and burrowed into the cushions. "This is my new favorite place in the entire world. I'm never going to leave this couch again."

"He's in shock. I'll get him some fluids." Celeste jumped off the couch and ran to the kitchen.

"Can you bring some food too?" Doug whimpered.

"Sure! I'll make a plate of snacks."

"Man, I don't remember Celeste ever being this nice. Did she get hit by lightning or somethin'?"

Zoe punched me in the arm.

Derek stared at me. "No, but I think something happened to *you* in New York that you forgot to tell me about."

I pulled the Triple T Token out of my shirt and twirled it around on the chain. "Um, yeah. There is this little thing."

"It's a little thing that makes *big* things happen," Zoe added as she pulled a hair tie from her wrist and put her hair up in a ponytail.

"Like taking us to *ancient Egypt*?" Derek leaned in closer to examine the token. "That was the SCARIEST but COOLEST thing that's ever happened to me."

"Stick around. More and better terrifying things await." Zoe rolled her eyes.

Derek turned his face to the front window and pulled his visor off his head. "Arcade, did any time pass while we were gone?"

I shrugged. "When we've gone through the doors before, we've always come back at the same time we left. Why?"

Derek slid off the couch and crawled on the floor. He stopped right under the window and peeked out. "That's what I was afraid of. The truck is still there."

"The truck?" Zoe crawled over next to Derek. "What truck?"

"The truck that's been following me ever since I took a post-it note with Arcade's name on it out of Mr. B's house."

"You're talkin' nonsense. And who's Mr. B?"

"He owns Forest Games and Golf. You know the guy. A little old and a lot grumpy."

Zoe ducked down lower. "Forest Games and Golf? This is getting creepy, Arcade . . ."

"Yeah, but it's finally making some sense! Derek, maybe we can see him better from *your* room." I rolled my shaky body off the couch and crawled to the hallway. "Zoe, stay here and help Celeste take care of Doug."

"Okay. I'll keep watching out this window. Let us know if you see anything down there."

Derek and I crawled to his room. "Arcade, we can't see anything better from my room."

"Shh. I know. But that will get us downstairs, and we can sneak out the back door, duck behind trees till we reach the other side of the cul-de-sac, and watch him from the woods."

Derek's eyes lit up. "That's brilliant! I knew everything would be okay once you got here."

"Yeah. I hope so. Just leave the bright yellow visor at home."

"Good idea. We'll go camo."

We quickly threw on some green and brown camo T-shirts and pulled Derek's camo net off his wall to cover us as we ran.

I pulled out my phone to make sure it was charged and ready for action. "He'll never know we're watching him. I'll log his license plate and other clues in my phone."

"Okay, dude, I gotcha covered!"

Derek and I snuck out of his room, tiptoed down the hallway, and gently opened the backyard screen door.

CREAK!

"Man, Derek, you gotta oil that door! I bet Zoe heard that."

Derek threw the net over both our heads. "Let's jam!"

It was just like the old days when Derek and I used to run away and hide from our sisters. But it was never because a truck was tailing us. And it was before I owned the Triple T Token.

Maybe this wasn't the greatest decision. But it *was* fun. And what could happen in our little neck of the woods?

"Arcade, you gotta slow down a little." Derek's taller than me, so he was having trouble keeping up since he had to bend his legs as he ran, to stay under the net.

"What if we crab-walk?" I suggested. "Then we can keep our eyes on the truck."

We flipped over and walked side-by-side on our hands and feet with our eyes peeking out of the net. We jetted between the trees, staying as low as we could. Derek's street is a cul-de-sac, so we were able to stay in the woods behind the houses and cross over to the truck side without stepping foot on the street.

"This is genius, Arcade." Derek huffed and puffed. "How close do you think we can get without him noticing?"

We crab-walked behind the house he was parked in

front of. Then we settled in behind a hedge and took some pictures.

"Ha! This is just like when we used to spy on Celeste and Zoe." I snapped some more pics, and then crawled out from under the net so I could get a picture of the truck's license plate.

"Be careful, Arcade."

And just as Derek said that, a guy opened the driver-side door of the truck and jumped out!

Derek hurried over to me and threw the net over my head. We both hit the ground. I was *sure* the guy saw, because he turned and jogged in our direction.

"That's him, all right. That's Mr. B."

I strained to see him through the netting. His head was covered with a hood, but I could see his face. He looked like the same guy who fought me on the street in New York. And the same guy who yelled at me at the arcade.

Is that Lenwood Badger? I thought he was in custody in New York City.

Mr. B slowed and approached the house where we were hiding behind the hedge.

"What do we do, Arcade?"

I couldn't think of anything, but . . .

"Run to the hideout!"

We dropped the net and ran to the place we always went when we were in trouble and didn't want anyone to find us. Inside the old, hollowed-out tree trunk, deep in the Cimarron neighborhood woods.

CHAPTER 13

Journey Box

It took us a minute to catch our breath.

"That . . ." Derek doubled over and put his hands on his knees, "was a close one."

"Too close. But no one will find us in here."

The log of the huge fallen tree had been a refuge anytime our moms were looking for us when we were little kids. Derek and I made a pact never to tell any grownups about the tree.

We climbed in a few feet. "I hope there are no biting ants in here." I pulled my phone out of my pocket and used the flashlight to see inside our hiding place. "Looks the same as the last time we were here. Hey, here's our tub of Red Vines!"

"Probably stale by now," Derek picked up the tub and shook it. The clump of Red Vines plopped around in one big glob.

"I bet Doug would eat 'em." I pointed to a wooden box that was hidden behind the tub. "What's that sittin' by the Red Vines?"

Derek reached over and brushed a bunch of bark off the top. He stared at it for moment before looking at me with wide eyes. "Dude, I think it's the journey box!"

"What? It is *not*! Let me see!"

Derek handed it over. I opened it. Inside was a bunch of envelopes.

"It *is* the journey box! I wonder how it got in *here*?"

"Beats me. I haven't seen this thing for a couple of years. I thought it was buried and lost somewhere."

"Here, hold my phone," I handed the phone with the light still on to Derek, and he shined it while I pulled out envelopes that represented all the years we were in elementary school. Each envelope held clues that the junior high kids left for us, so we could find treasures in the Cimarron woods. The clues also included encouraging and challenging words to help us through life. It was a super fun neighborhood game that we all played every summer, and Derek and I looked forward to the day when we would be the junior highers who would leave the notes. But then I moved, and the box was lost. Or so I thought.

"What's *that* one?" Derek shined the light on a gold envelope that stood out from the tattered white ones. It didn't have a year written on it, but it looked like it was stuffed full of notes!

I lifted the envelope out of the box, and the Triple T Token heated up. I put my hand to my heart.

Not now. Not without Zoe here.

The token cooled. But my hands holding the envelope warmed up. I turned the envelope over and lifted the flap. I pulled out a folded paper that had the number one printed on it. I opened it up and read:

> ### Hole number one: The journey starts with a humble heart.

"Hole number one?" Derek scratched his head. "What's that?"

I stared at the words for a few seconds. The token lay right against my pounding heart, and my stomach churned.

I know.

"It's hole one of the windmill course at Forest Games and Golf."

"The windmill course? That thing's all broken down. How could a journey start there? And what kind of journey?"

"I don't know. But we have to go there and find out."

CHAPTER 14

Sister Wrath

Zoe and Celeste were waiting for us in the backyard of 2300 Cimarron Road.

"Get in here!" Celeste grabbed Derek by the ear and pulled. "You two gave us a heart attack. First you show us some stalker truck and then you disappear! What kind of stupid trick was that?"

"We had a *deal*, Arcade." My sister didn't have to say anything else.

I know, I know, Zoe. We promised to never be out of each other's sight unless we were at school, in case the token acts up.

"I'm sorry, Zoe. I just wanted to spy on the truck. I didn't know we'd be running from the guy into the woods."

"INTO THE WOODS? He could have caught you and . . . hurt you or something."

I held out the journey box. "But we found *this*."

"Is that what I think it is?" Celeste swept her hand across the top of the box.

"Is that what she thinks it is?" I guess Doug decided to leave the couch after all.

"It's exactly what she . . . you think it is, Celeste," said Derek. "The journey box! It was in our . . . uh . . . it was out there in the trees. Found after all this time."

"And it had a gold envelope inside." I pulled it out of my pocket. "With clues. Zoe, the clues have something to do with the token. I can feel it." I touched my hand to my shirt where the token hung beneath it. It was warm, but in a soothing way, like a heating pad.

"Alright," said Celeste, in a huff. "Y'all get in the house." She opened the screen door.

CREAK!!!

Celeste cringed. "Derek! When are you gonna oil this thing?"

CHAPTER 15

Clueing Them In

Tell us *everything*." Celeste led us all to the couch, where we sat in a circle, the journey box in the middle.

"Yeah, tell us everything." Doug sat next to Celeste, munching on a bowl of cereal.

I told them everything I knew. The old lady at the library. The adventures we'd been on so far. The trip to the past where Zoe and I watched our parents win the token and then disappear.

"And that's pretty much it up to now. Except Egypt, and you were all there with us. But you didn't see the lady."

Zoe bounced on the couch. "You saw her *again*? Did she say anything?"

"We had a short conversation. She said that the travel guide knows where we're going, and we find out the 'why' after we go."

Zoe narrowed her eyes. "NOT helpful."

"And she said that a pyramid is a square, so I guess she thinks like me."

Zoe threw her arms up. "Of *course*."

"And, speaking of *courses*! Check this OUT!" I opened the journey box, pulled out the golden envelope, and showed everyone the clue. "I'm sure it's talking about hole one of the windmill course at Forest Games and Golf."

Zoe read it out loud. "'Hole number one: The journey starts with a humble heart'? It's a stretch, but worth looking into." Then she frowned. "But how are we going to get over there with this Mr. B watching our every move?"

"He can't be *there* all the time. He was *here* just a little while ago." I snuck over to look out the window. The truck was gone. "We know what he drives, so we can keep an eye out for that."

"And we know where he lives, so I say we turn the tables and spy on *him*!" Derek had popped his yellow visor back on his head.

"Wait!" Zoe stuck out a hand. "What do you mean, we know where he lives?"

Derek's eyes shifted over to mine, and then back to Zoe. "Well, *I* do. I helped him move in."

"Where does he live?" Celeste narrowed her eyes at Derek.

"Yeah, where does he live?" repeated Doug.

"He lives at the end of the street."

"WHAT street?" Celeste crunched her eyebrows together.

Derek swallowed hard. "Our street. Four houses down. 2292 Cimarron Road."

Zoe gasped. "We're going to be spending a month here! And that guy is right on the corner? How are we supposed to go in and out knowing he's there?"

Derek cleared his throat. "He's got a few video cams out there too."

"So we just grin and say cheese as we go by." Doug smiled big.

Celeste pushed her brother over. "Derek! Why did you help him?"

"I didn't know he was possibly some bad guy! I thought he was just the guy from the arcade. And I *still* don't know what's goin' on. I just found a post-it in his house with Arcade's name on it."

"He wants the Triple T Token. He's not going to get it. It belongs to me."

"I think it belonged to *him* first," Zoe said.

"But the old lady says it's mine now. I don't understand why, but maybe we'll find out if we go check out hole one at Forest Games and Golf. Anyone up for a game?"

CHAPTER 16

Suspicious Fivesome

orry, Loop, remember what the sign said? No dogs allowed."

Woof!

I ruffled Loopy's fur and placed him behind the dog gate in Derek's room. "We'll see you soon, boy."

I brushed dog hair off my hands and grabbed my wallet from Derek's desk. "Okay, let's do this thing! And instead of a bright visor, maybe you should wear a dark ball cap."

We *all* wore hats. And baggy jackets. Luckily, it was drizzly, so it wouldn't seem out of the ordinary.

Derek snuck out the front door so he could spy down the street. "The truck is there now, so if we go around the cul-de-sac, through the woods on the other side, we can sneak out of the street from behind Miss Gertrude's house without his video camera catching us."

"Miss Gertrude is *still* alive?"

Miss Gertrude was an old lady when I was little! She would sit in her rocking chair, out on her porch, and hold her hands up in the air, praying for us kids in the neighborhood. I know because whenever I would be over playing with Derek, Miss Gertrude would wave from across the street and say, "Arcade Livingston, I'm praying for you, son! God's got great plans for you!" And then she would just keep on waving.

"Yep, she's still there," Derek said. "She doesn't sit out as much anymore, but she's out there a lot."

"I wonder if she knows about Mr. B across the street?"

"Yeah, she does. She was watching when we were unloading things. She had her hands up, praying. Mr. B said she was a crazy old lady."

"Maybe we can get her to help us in some way."

A spy in a rocking chair. I thought, *That's the best kind of spy! But can we trust her with our information?*

We were huffing and puffing after our three-mile hike from the Cimarron woods to Forest Games and Golf.

"I'm glad Aunt Weeda is picking us up." Zoe panted as she bent over to catch her breath. "This town needs a subway."

We walked to the arcade entrance. "Okay," I said, "let's split up, but play next to each other. Girls in a group, boys in a group. Pretend we don't know each other."

"That will be pleasant." Zoe walked by and flicked me in the shoulder.

"Very funny, whatever your name is. And we need a signal if we see anything suspicious."

"How about we turn our caps around? Bill to the back." Derek has a way with hats.

"Sounds good to me," I said.

We went into acting mode, pretending we didn't know the girls. "Ladies, first!" I gestured to Celeste and Zoe to go ahead of us in the mini-golf line.

"That will be six dollars each." The clerk, a teenage boy, smiled at Zoe. "And the clubs are behind you. Let me know if you have any questions." His eye fluttered like Jacey's did in the bakery.

What's with all the eye trouble in this town?

Zoe tilted her head and grinned. "Thank you very much." Then she and Celeste turned to get their clubs. She bumped my shoulder. "Hey, kid, watch yourself!" Then she walked on.

You are enjoying this way too much.

Derek, Doug, and I paid for our games, picked up our clubs, and headed out to the windmill course. The windmill lay on its side over the creek, just as I always remembered it.

"This place is a dump," Doug said as he experimented with his grip on the putter. "Why don't they fix it up?"

I looked over the drab surroundings and shrugged. "Don't know."

And then the token heated up. I stopped in my tracks. The last thing I wanted was for the doors to appear here, now, at Forest Games and Golf. I grabbed for the bill of my cap, and almost turned it, when the token cooled back down.

Whew!

The girls sat on the bench at hole one, looking up the hill at the fallen windmill. Zoe checked her scorecard. "Keeping score is a joke." She printed her name on the scorecard. "You can't control where these balls go. If I hit my ball in the trough up there where the windmill used to stand, it's going to roll through the pipes and pop out behind a barrier. And from there, it's like eight shots before you get it in the hole. It makes no sense at all."

Celeste placed her ball on the starting mat. "Maybe this game will be different. I'm gonna close my eyes." She shut her eyes tight then smacked the ball. It flew up, bounced over the fake blue grass, and hit the fallen windmill, getting stuck in one of the blades.

The boys and I laughed.

Zoe gave us the stink-eye. "That was a nice shot, Celeste. You can chip it into the hole from there." The hole was down the hill from where the broken-down windmill was resting. Zoe placed her ball on the mat and smacked it right in the trough.

We waited and watched as the ball rolled through the pipes to the bottom level and popped out on the wrong side of the barrier.

Zoe placed her putter on her shoulder. "Yep, I've seen this all before."

"Try not to take too long getting it in the hole and holding up everyone's game."

She glared over at me. "I don't *know* you and I don't care."

I grinned and placed my ball on the mat. But then the token heated up again. So did the envelope in my pocket! I stepped away from my ball. "Hang on, guys," I said through gritted teeth. I scanned the course for video cameras, then hid behind a bush so I could pull out the envelope and read the first clue again.

> ## Hole number one: The journey starts with a humble heart.

And then it hit me.

I know what I have to do.

I folded up the envelope, put it back in my pocket, and picked up my ball. "You guys go before me."

"Ah, man, a gentleman!" Doug smiled and placed his ball on the mat. He chipped it in the creek, watched the ripples in the water for a moment, and then grabbed his belly. "This game is making me hungry."

"No food till we round the corner at the tenth hole," Derek said as he set his ball, took a second to line it up, and then putted it perfectly into the trough.

A few seconds later, Zoe hollered from the green below. "Hey! You didn't wait for us to putt out! You hit my ball!"

"Oops! Sorry!" Derek looked down the hill at the girls. "Looks like my ball is behind the barrier too."

"There has to be a way for a ball to end up on the correct the side of the barrier." I took a hike up the hill.

As I approached the windmill, the token heated up a little. How did this thing fall, and why had no one bothered to pull it back up? It's clearly one of the most noticeable attractions here.

I walked on the fake grass and stared inside the trough. Sure enough, there was one *skinny* tube right in the center. That had to be the one that would spit you out on the right side of the barrier. Most would fall into the wider tubes on either side of it, ending up on . . . Zoe's side.

"Okay, Doug, I see what you have to do! Fish your ball out of the creek and try again! You have to putt it perfectly straight!"

Doug scratched his head. "Perfectly straight?"

"That's what I said."

He sniffed and shook his head around. "Okay, then, here we gooooooo!" He jogged over to the creek, pulled out the ball, put it down on the mat, and hit it pretty hard. And crooked! I snatched it off the grass, walked over to the trough, and dropped it in the skinny tube.

"Hey! Isn't that cheating?" This from the guy who I let have a do-over after hitting in the creek.

"Doug! This isn't the PGA tour! I wanna see what happens!"

Doug ran down the hill to where the girls and Derek were putting out. Just as Zoe was lifting her ball out of the hole, Doug's ball came dribbling out on the correct side of the barrier, rolled a few feet, and plunked into the hole.

"Hole-in-one!" I held both hands in the air. "Way to go, Dougie!"

Doug took his hat off and bowed for the crowd.

The girls shook their heads and took off to the next hole. After all, they weren't supposed to know us.

"Hit your ball, Arcade!" Derek watched from above.

"In a minute. I have to check something out." I made my way over to the windmill. Its base lay exposed to the elements, and the top with the wind blades lay on the other side of the small man-made creek. It was hollow inside and didn't seem like it would be that difficult to pull back up. I looked under it and tried to rock it with my arms. It wouldn't budge.

"Okay, you're heavier than I thought. But not too much for a small crane to lift." I walked around the back of it and, as I did, a flash of light caught my eye. The token flared back. "What was that?" The light flashed again. I followed its beam to a gold plaque bolted to the windmill. I leaned closer and used my jacket sleeve to wipe the dirt off. It had a word etched into it in bold letters:

Humility

And underneath the word humility, there were small words . . . *Arcade Adventures*.

I pulled the clue out of my pocket and stared at it.

Hole number one: The journey starts with a humble heart.

I took out my phone and snapped a picture of the plaque.

"Arcade, are you gonna take your turn?" Derek came running up alongside me. "Did ya find somethin?"

I scratched my head. "Maybe." I pointed to the plaque.

Derek read it. "Humility, huh? Seems to match the clue. But what does it mean?"

"You got me. What does humility mean to you, Derek?"

Derek put his hand to his chest. "You're askin' *me*? You're the word guy."

"You must have some idea."

"Hmmm." Derek rubbed his chin. "Humility means not acting like you're all that, but treating others like they are?"

I stared at Derek. "That's profound."

"Oh, good. What does profound mean?"

"Profound. Showing great knowledge or insight."

Derek stood up a little straighter. "Oh. Thanks!"

"I think this course has some kind of life lesson hidden in it. And humility is at the start of it. At the start of the course . . . wait a minute! At the start of a journey? If you don't think you're all that, that means you're willing to learn . . . the journey starts with a humble heart!"

"Cool." Derek scratched his chin. "But what does that have to do with the token?"

I grasped the token under my shirt. "I don't know."

"Maybe the other clues in the golden envelope will tell you." Derek's smile turned to a frown as he looked behind my shoulder toward something in the distance. "Uh-oh."

"What's going on?"

Derek slumped down. "The truck just pulled in."

"Oh, man! We gotta tell the girls and get outta here!" We ran down the hill where Doug was now playing golf with Zoe and Celeste.

"So you finally decided to join us?" Zoe was lining up her shot on the mat of the second hole.

"We gotta go. Mr. B just pulled up!"

Zoe turned and looked toward the parking lot. "He's coming this way. Quick, let's go through the arcade."

We grabbed our clubs and hurried through the front entrance. Now *this* was the arcade I remembered. A few old games, plinking away, and the smell of stale pizza lingering in the air. Small groups of kids hung out and talked in different areas of the dark room. A couple of kids were playing ping-pong with worn-out paddles, and players at the air hockey table had to hit the puck harder because the air vents didn't work. It certainly was not the same place it had been when it was called Arcade Adventures.

"Derek, can you call your mom to see if she can pick us up early?" I watched the front door like a hawk for any sign of Mr. B.

"Nah, she'll get mad if I bother her. Maybe *you* should call her, Arcade. You're her favorite nephew."

I pulled out my phone and poked the contact button to pull up Aunt Weeda's number. But for some reason, when I did that, my phone started dialing . . . The Bridgeview Bakery!

"NO! That's *not* what I wanted to do!"

The phone only rang once. "Bridgeview Bakery. This is Jacey. How can I help you?"

Oh no, oh no, oh no, oh no! I just called a GIRL!

"Hello? Is this Arcade Livingston?"

And she has caller id!

"Um . . . hello, Jacey."

"Hey, Arcade. Do you need more bread already?"

"Uhhhhhhh . . . no . . . I . . . uhhhhhhh . . ."

Derek grabbed the phone. "Hey, Jacey. He called because he needs a ride home."

Derek! What are you saying? That's not true! Well, it is true, BUT . . .

He handed the phone back to me. I held it to my ear. "Ride . . . home. Yeeeeaaaah. That's what we need."

"Oh, that's easy! Mom and I are just closing up. Where are you?"

"I'm sure it's way too far . . ."

Jacey giggled. "You're too funny. This is Forest, Virginia. The town is the size of a postage stamp."

Derek grabbed the phone again. "We're at Forest Games and Golf. There's five of us. Do you have a big car?"

"You bet! We've got an SUV that seats eight! We'll be there in ten minutes."

My mouth suddenly lost all its saliva. Jacey—the cute girl—was coming to pick us up!

This. Is. Not. Happening.

"Good thinking to call Jacey!" Derek gave me a high-five. "Mom's not off work for another hour anyway."

Zoe punched me in the arm and winked uncontrollably. "Yeah, good *thinking,* Arcade."

Heat radiated from my neck up into my hair, causing sweat to run down my forehead, my glasses to fog up, and my red frames to slide down my nose.

This is worse than what the token does to me.

"Hey! Is that *him*?" Celeste whispered and pointed over to the golf counter. Mr. B was talking to the teenage boy who sold us our golf games.

"We can't go out the door now. He'll see us." She put her finger to her lips. "Follow me." Zoe led us back to the corner by the claw machine—the same place where we had spied on Mom and Dad when they won the token.

The claw machine was still there, but it was turned off and only had a few stuffed animals in it. One of them was the green and yellow cockatoo!

"Poor Milo. No one wants you and your annoyin—"

Right then, the claw machine came to life! Lights flashed and the claw shot up and down. It knocked the few animals around and music blared, attracting the attention of all the kids in the arcade.

"Arcade, what did you do?" Zoe pointed to the Triple T Token. It was flashing inside my shirt. "We have to get out of here!"

I checked above our heads for glitter clouds, but there were none.

This would be a great time for the coin slot and the doors to appear . . .

I popped my head around the corner. No Mr. B in sight.

"Let's go." I made a beeline for the side door.

Please, let Jacey's SUV be there.

I took the longest strides I could and practically leapt through the doorway, hoping everyone was following me.

"ARCADE! I KNEW you'd return!" A deep, scary voice echoed over the Forest Games and Golf loudspeaker.

Chills shot down my spine and I froze right there in the parking lot. "Did you guys hear that?"

"Hear what?" Zoe stood at my side, her hand on my shoulder. "I didn't hear anything."

This is not good. Where is Jacey? We need her NOW!

I felt a finger tap on my other shoulder. "Hi."

I jumped about a mile. It was her. And she was holding what looked like a full bakery bag.

"We're parked right over here." Jacey pointed to a red Suburban with the name "Bridgeview Bakery" painted on the door. It was pulled right up to the side entrance. "Y'all can climb on in. I'll be right back." She took off toward the arcade, the bakery bag swinging back and forth in her hand as she walked.

"Now, where's she goin'?" Derek looked puzzled as we made our way to the SUV. "I hope she doesn't run into Mr. B and give away our location."

I watched her walk in the door, her smile brighter than any of the lights in the run-down old arcade. "Something tells me she won't." I walked up to the rolled down, driver's side window. A woman I had seen somewhere before smiled and greeted me.

"Hello, Arcade. Jacey told me you were back in Virginia for a visit."

"Hello."

Where do I know you from?

The lady jumped out of the SUV and greeted everyone else. "Wow, look at how you've all grown! Do you remember me?"

The girls stepped in closer. Zoe spoke. "Mrs. Green? From Sunday school?"

The lady smiled. "You remembered! Yes! I taught you all in the elementary class a few years back. Arcade and Derek were just little guys then." She turned to Doug. "I don't think I know you, though."

"I'm Doug. Arcade's new friend from New York."

The lady's eyes lit up. "It's a delight to meet you."

"So, what happened?" Celeste shoved her hands in her pockets. "Why aren't you at church anymore?"

"I'm still there. When my husband and I opened the bakery, we had to switch to the Sunday night service." She laughed. "People have to have their donuts in the morning."

"You got that right!" Doug rubbed his belly.

Mrs. Green turned to me. "Jacey *always* used to talk about that nice little boy with the special name. Ahhhcade. She couldn't say her r's very well back then, and she liked you because you never made fun of her like some of the other kids."

Okay, now I remembered the little girl from Sunday school. She was crying one day because someone said she talked funny. I gave her my snack. It was all I could think of to do. I never did know what happened to her. Till now.

Just then, Jacey exited Forest Games and Golf and walked to the SUV. Empty handed.

CHAPTER 17

Cinnamon Ride

I hope you kids don't mind a little detour before I take you home." Mrs. Green gestured toward the back of the SUV. "I have a few baked goods to deliver."

"Baked goods? What kind of baked goods?" Doug breathed in deep, hogging all the cinnamon aroma out of the air.

Mrs. Green laughed. "Anything we have left over at the end of the day, we deliver to places around town. Depending on how much we have, we visit the homeless shelter, a senior center, and an apartment complex where we know there are people who don't have much money for groceries."

"That's cool," Celeste said. "It looks like you have a huge pile back there. Was business slow today?"

"No way," Jacey turned from her shotgun position to face us. "We were hopping! We usually make more than we know we'll sell, so that we'll have some to give."

"That's so thoughtful," Zoe said. "You must be such a blessing to those people."

"No, they're a blessing to us." Mrs. Green smiled back

at us in the rearview. "I love all our Bridgeview Bakery customers, but this is the highlight of my day. This is what makes running the business worthwhile."

It was a comfortable feeling, riding along in the Suburban filled with cinnamon smells. I sat back and felt relaxed for the first time all day.

"So, did you find Mr. Badger and give him his bread?" Mrs. Green glanced over at Jacey.

Mr. Badger?

"Yes. I told him to have a great day and that we'd be back to visit next week. He said thanks, and he kind of smiled."

"We're wearing him down." Mrs. Green turned back to us. "He lost his wife many years ago to cancer. The cinnamon bread was their favorite, so we always save a loaf for him and try to bring it by on Saturday afternoons."

"I always wondered why an owner of a business for kids was so grouchy," I said.

"Oh, it goes back even further than that." Mrs. Green shook her head. "Not sure what happened. Seems like it started when that windmill fell down . . ."

"Here we are!" Jacey pointed to a long, white building. "Forest Memory Care. The people don't always remember me, but they are as sweet as pie." Jacey's cheeks were rosy, and her eyes beamed.

Mrs. Green parked the SUV and opened the driver's side door. "We'll be back in a few minutes, then we'll take you home. Your street is on our way to the homeless shelter."

"Ah, here we are! 2300 Cimarron Road. Derek, tell your mom to stop in the bakery soon and I'll give her a dozen donuts."

"Oh, yeah, we're comin' tomorrow, baby!" Doug jumped out of the back seat.

Mrs. Green laughed. "Tomorrow would be just fine. You kids, don't be strangers, okay?"

"Yeah," Jacey added. "Don't go back to New York without saying goodbye, Arcade."

She smiled at me, and my cheeks heated up. At least it wasn't the token. It had been a long day, and I wasn't ready for another travel adventure.

"Thanks again for the ride!" Derek waved, and we all watched as the cinnamon-scented Suburban turned around at the cul-de-sac and headed back out toward the end of the street.

CHAPTER 18
Sprinkler Heads

The next day was Sunday, so Aunt Weeda was home. We all went to church together, and then spent the afternoon snacking, watching movies, and playing football and Frisbee in the backyard. The golden envelope sat on the nightstand in Derek's bedroom. Every time I thought about reading the rest of the clues, Aunt Weeda showed up with another activity for us.

"Anyone want to play Monopoly?" Aunt Weeda brought out the gameboard after dinner.

Who can pass on Monopoly?

So we played and played and played, until we all crawled to our beds, half asleep, at about 1:00 am.

When we woke up the next "morning" at noon, Aunt Weeda was already gone. She left Celeste a voicemail on her phone: "This would be a great day for y'all to mow the lawn and weed. Tell Derek to please fix the broken sprinkler heads in the garden. We're floodin' out our tomato plants!"

Zoe stretched and leaned back on the living room couch. "I like it here. Things seem normal. It might be nice to enjoy the Virginia air, even if we are cleaning up the yard."

"Do you know how to fix a sprinkler head, Derek?" I turned to my cousin in the kitchen, where us guys were eating cereal for lunch.

"Oh, yeah. I've fixed almost all the sprinklers at least once." Derek and Celeste's parents are divorced, and his dad doesn't make it over to the house very often. So Derek has to fix things, since his mom is always working. Good thing he's handy.

We inhaled our cereal and had some cinnamon bread for dessert. That gave us the energy we needed to put on some grubby clothes and attack the big backyard job.

"I'll mow," Doug said. "I don't have grass at my house, so this is cool!" He made his way over to the mower in the side yard, where Derek showed him how to start it up.

Celeste and Zoe put on flowery floppy hats and gardening gloves. "We got the weeds," Celeste called as she took Zoe with her to the far corner of the yard.

"Okay, Arcade," Derek said, popping on his bright yellow visor, "that makes you my assistant. Grab a shovel and we'll take out some of this grass around the sprinkler head. We'll pull the broken one off, snap the new one on, and we'll be in business!"

"We doin' this!" I followed Doug to the first broken

sprinkler. I dug the shovel into the ground. Then I jumped on it, because I don't like to do things halfway.

The shovel dug in deep, but crooked. I fell back and watched as a huge geyser shot up from the ground. It took me a second before I realized what the yellow thing was that was getting pummeled around in the spray of water. It was Derek's visor.

"Duuuuuude! What's goin' on?" I lay there on the ground, getting soaked.

"Arcaaaaade! What did you do?" Zoe came running over. Funny how she automatically blamed *me* for the problem.

Celeste arrived next, pulling the brim of her floppy hat down on each side of her face. "Derek, didn't you turn the water off?"

"NO! I DIDN'T TURN IT OFF! I WAS GOING TO DO IT AFTER WE DUG THE HOLE."

I sat up and watched Derek struggle to stop the water flow from the pipe with his hands. He wasn't having much luck. A stream blasted him in the center of his forehead. I turned my head to see Doug, mowing away on the other side of the yard, bopping to the music in his earbuds.

"FLOODING! WE'VE GOT FLOODING, PEOPLE!"

"WELL, YOU CAN'T STOP IT WITH YOUR HAND, DEREK!"

"I KNOW, CELESTE!!!!"

Water sprayed everywhere! It would have been a hilarious sight except that, if we didn't do something soon, we were going to turn Aunt Weeda's beautiful yard into a grassy swamp.

"GO TURN OFF THE WATER, DEREK!" Celeste grabbed him by the collar and pulled him up on his feet.

I just sat there, laughing and getting more soaked, until the token heated up and the water turned to glitter.

Doug, finally getting a clue that something crazy was happening, ran over.

"WATER and GLITTER! Arcade, where we goin'?"

I stood up and tried to brush glitter off my wet pants, as streams of the little, gold, papery squares continued to shoot out of the sprinkler head like a firework fountain on the 4th of July.

"I don't know how to turn *that* off!" Derek ran over to his visor, which lay a few feet away, and he pulled it on his head. "Do you, Arcade?"

Celeste shook her wet hands. "I can't go anywhere looking like this!"

The glitter shooting out from the sprinkler formed into golden doors, and a golden coin slot appeared before our eyes. It pulsed light straight into my chest.

"You guys want to go somewhere and dry off?"

"Well, you never know. We might end up at the bottom of the Atlantic." Zoe gave me a cross-eyed stare.

I nodded. "I promise not to pick *ocean*."

I pulled the token out from under my shirt. The thing was blazing hot! It singed my thumb and then shot from my hand into the coin slot.

"UP or DOWN?"

Why is this my choice? Every. Time.

"NOT UP!" Doug hugged the back wall of the elevator. "I can't handle up. Please, not up."

"No need to worry, Doug." Zoe wiped water off her drippy chin. "Arcade *never* picks one of the options. Do you, bro?"

Well, *that* was a challenge, if I ever heard one! I couldn't let Zoe start predicting my actions. This time, I'd pick one of the options . . . sort of.

"Okay, Doug, we're not going up. We're going to go . . . LOW!"

I punched the one red button with the heel of my hand, and the elevator floor dropped out from under us.

"AAAAAAAAAAAAAAAAHHHHHHHHHHHHH!"

CHAPTER 19

The Low Life

I'm sitting on mushy ground. Much like we just left in Derek's soggy backyard. But a quick look around confirms one thing: we're not in Virginia anymore.

"What's with all the windmills?" Derek's visor is a little bent now. His head probably hit the elevator ceiling just as hard as mine did when we dropped . . . low.

"Is this Holland?" I look around and compare the scene to a picture in a travel book I read at the library.

"It's called the *Netherlands*," Zoe pushes herself up from the spongy grass.

"It's called the *Netherlands*?" Doug stands up and scans the territory. "I hope they have food. And . . . I think I left the mower running back at home. Is that a bad thing?"

"It means more broken sprinkler heads." Derek shakes his head and adjusts his visor. "The place is gonna be flooded when we get back."

"Why do you think the token brought us *here*?" Zoe starts walking toward the windmill in the distance.

"The lady said that we don't find out the *why* until after

104

we go." I stand up and brush the wet grass from the seat of my pants before following Zoe.

"All I know is this is the *best* summer ever." Celeste straightens her floppy hat and runs to catch up to Zoe. "I'm so glad you guys came back to Virginia."

The closest windmill to us has an information kiosk out in front.

Cool. I love reading about faraway places.

WELCOME TO HOLLAND, it says on the table display. I make sure I point *that* out to Zoe. She pokes me in the ribs on my ticklish side, making me jump.

Zoe begins to read out loud:

"The windmills of Holland served many purposes. The most important was to pump floodwater out of the lowlands and transport it back to the rivers beyond the dikes."

"We're in the *low*lands! I chose LOW in the elevator. That's DOPE!"

"Ahem." Zoe continues. "Without the windmills, the people of Holland would have had no land to live on or farm. Eventually, windmills were also used to grind grain and saw wood. There are over 1,000 windmills in Holland."

"That's a lot of windmills," Derek says.

"Hey, look over there!" Celeste points to a large banner that says, "National Mill Day." Next to the banner is a long line of bicycles for rent.

"We've arrived on a special day." I walk toward the bike rental. "Anyone want to go for a ride?"

The young blonde girl manning the bicycle rental gives

us a funny look as we approach. After all, we're soaked and wearing gardening clothes, emerging from the marsh land.

I pretend like I'm a regular tourist. "Hello, we're here to celebrate National Mill Day."

She shakes her head. "Sorry, that was yesterday. You missed it."

"WHAT?"

She jumps back.

"Oh, I'm sorry. I didn't mean to startle you. I'm just surprised. Are you sure we missed it? Our tour guide wouldn't miss something that important."

"Where are you from?"

"We've come all the way from Virginia in the United States." Zoe takes off her gardening hat and smiles her biggest smile. "Is there any way we can see inside one of these beautiful windmills?" My sister can be charming when she wants to be.

The girl turns to look back at the windmill behind her. "I just work the bike rentals. But if you wait here a minute, I'll see if Stephan can help you."

"Stephan," Doug says. "That sounds like someone who knows windmills!"

The girl disappears for a few minutes and comes back with a middle-aged man wearing a tweed cap. He gives us an even stranger look than she did.

"Hello. Anna tells me you are all from . . . Virginia? And how is it that your tour guide missed National Mill Day? It is listed on the Internet and is widely known all throughout the Netherlands."

"*Netherlands*, huh?" Zoe smirks in my direction. "I like this guy."

"Sir, is there a way that my friends and I could take a closer look at one of these windmills? There must be a reason why we landed . . . er . . . uh, that our tour guide brought us here."

Stephan looks beyond us. "Where is this tour guide of yours?"

"Oh, he went away for now. He'll be back. Sometime." I feel for the empty chain around my neck.

Stephan nods. "All right, then. Far be it from me to turn away curious young people all the way from . . . Virginia." He crunches his eyebrows together. "Follow me!"

Our group follows Stephan toward the enormous blue windmill. It looks a lot like the one laying in the creek at Forest Games and Golf, only much larger.

"Man, these "Hollandites" are *nice*," Doug whispers as he crowds in next to me on the path leading to the windmill. "Do you think they have good food here?"

"We'll find out later, if we stay that long. For now, keep your eyes and ears open for clues."

"What kinds of clues?" Derek asks.

"I don't know." I pull out my phone to show them the picture I took of the golden plaque on the windmill at Forest Games and Golf. The screen shows nothing but glitter. *Ugh!* I shake my head.

"Humility. Look for humility."

"You missed the festivities yesterday. The decorations, the games, the pancakes . . ." Stephan leads us up the small step and inside the large windmill.

"Pancakes? I missed the pancakes?" Doug's shoulders droop.

I pat him on the back. "That's what the man said, Doug."

When we get through the door, we gather in a small area in the center of the room, and Stephan explains how the windmill works.

"This mill was used to pump water out of the marsh into the river so we could have farmland. Much of Holland is below sea level, you know. We are always fighting the water. Now we have fancy pumps to get rid of the water, but these humble windmills started it all and made it possible for the Dutch to live successful lives."

"*Humble*?" I'm all ears now.

Stephan grins. "Did I say humble?" He looks up and scratches his cheek. "I suppose I meant simple. Only people can exhibit humility, isn't that the truth? But I sometimes look at these windmills as old friends who stayed low so our people could be lifted up."

I'm stunned. The man said the word *humility*!

Stephan sighs. "This windmill you're standing in has just been restored. It had a cracked cap so the blades couldn't turn. It took two years for the community to raise the money needed to replace the sail frame structure and the turning system. Yesterday, we powered her up for the first time and celebrated her return during National Mill Day."

"And you celebrated with pancakes?" Doug pats his belly.

"Yes, we did, young man." Stephan's eyes gleam. "Say, would you like me to crank her up?"

"Can you *do* that?" Zoe bounces on her toes. "I would love to see it."

Stephan's eyes shift left, then right, and then he winks. "Looks like I'm in charge right now. So why not put on a show for my new Virginia friends?"

He begins the process of getting the blades going. It's a spectacular sight! Wheels turn, cranking up buckets that slosh water up, and over . . . somewhere.

"All from the power of wind," Derek says. "Amazing!"

"And that . . ." Stephan stands proudly, "is how we were able to farm instead of drown!" He chuckles. "These mills were worth more than gold to us."

Something thumps on my chest. It's gold. And it's hot.

Oh, no. I gotta get everyone out of here!

"Stephan, dude, thank you so much! This windmill is spectacular. We gotta go, though. Our tour guide is waiting . . ."

"Some tour guide," Doug says. "We missed the pancakes."

"It's been a pleasure meeting all of you. Ha, I guess I didn't catch your names." Stephan leads us out of the windmill. "Come again next year. But come a day earlier!"

He takes off his cap and waves as the others follow my lead, jogging back to . . . I'm not sure where yet. The token is back on my chain, but where are the doors?

We walk for a half mile or so, down a road that cuts through the countryside. It's cool outside, but that blazing token on my chest is making me sweat.

"Are we stuck in the Netherlands?" Zoe asks. "If so, I'd like to find some tulip fields."

"I'd like to find some food," Doug adds.

"I agree with Doug." Celeste pulls off her goofy hat and smiles at him.

I stare at the road ahead. "Humility . . . humility . . . hmmm."

Derek waves a hand in front of my face. "You okay, dog?"

I stop and turn around to look at the windmill again, its blades turning, making it seem alive.

What did Stephan say? Ah, yes! It's simple, but worth more than gold.

"Guys, I think I'm supposed to fix the windmill."

Zoe comes alongside me. "See those blades turning? It's fixed. I think that token is burning up your brain cells."

I shake my head. "No. I'm not supposed to fix *that* one. I'm supposed to fix the windmill at Forest Games and Golf."

All of a sudden, there are tulips in the fields. But they're not red, yellow, and orange. They are gold. Covered in glitter.

Celeste gasps and runs out in the middle of them. "Zoe, take a picture of me!"

Zoe shakes her head. "It won't work, trust me!" But

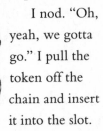

we all stop for a minute and take in the view—windmills in the background with a field of gold in front. Golden elevator doors rise up from the field, and in front is the coin slot.

"Do we have to go back so soon?" Celeste asks. "I feel like a better person here."

I nod. "Oh, yeah, we gotta go." I pull the token off the chain and insert it into the slot.

The doors open and we step in. I can't wait to get back.

I have a mission to repair a windmill.

We landed in Derek's backyard in mud.

Where's that humble windmill now that we need it?

The sprinkler head was still pumping water sky high, soaking the vegetable garden and patio, and creating lakes and rivers in the grass.

Somehow Zoe landed with her face in the direct line of

the spray, which put her in a mood. "I'm going in to take a shower. I'm soooo DONE here." She stomped off.

Celeste ran in after her. But before she did, she gave Derek a look. "You better have this under control before Mom gets home." Then she checked the time on her phone. "You've got one hour." She put out her hand and swirled it around in the air. "So, just DO what you need to DO!"

Now that's the Celeste I know!

Derek, Doug, and I stood there in the middle of the mayhem. It felt like we were at the water park. And it would have been fun if we *were* at the water park.

"I guess we should start by turning the water off." Derek ran for the side of the house. Doug and I followed. "I can't remember which knob it is, so let's just turn them all off."

That was a great idea, except for the fact that we turned the water off to the whole house. And Zoe was trying to take a shower.

Yeeeeaaah. She didn't talk to us the rest of the night.

I couldn't sleep. My mind wouldn't turn off. I had so many questions in my head—which wasn't new for me, but now I had just enough information to confuse the sleep right out of me.

This must be how detectives feel.

As I snuck out of Derek's room, I grabbed the golden envelope from my nightstand. I almost kicked Loopy, who was blocking the door. I lifted him and snuggled him up to my neck. "I gotta figure out what to do, Loop." I tiptoed into the living room, plopped down on the couch in the dark, and bonked heads with something.

"Owww." It was Zoe. "Arcade, what are you doing out here in the middle of the night?" Zoe turned on the little lamp on the corner table next to the couch.

"I couldn't sleep, and I didn't want to wake up Derek with all my tossing and turning."

She scooted over and threw me a pillow. "Same. Didn't want to wake Celeste."

I crawled over the ottomans and took a place next to

her. She had a huge blanket, so I pulled some of it over on me. Loopy crawled up on my lap and promptly fell asleep. "Zoe, do you think it's time to call Mom and Dad and tell them everything?"

Zoe thought for a minute. "They're busy, Arcade. I wouldn't want to worry them till we know what's really up. They might make us go back to New York. And I really like hanging out with Celeste."

My sister had been having a really hard few weeks in New York. She's not the kind of person to talk about things unless she's really concerned or hurting, so I knew things were bad when she confided in me that she hadn't made any friends at her new high school yet.

"Do you have a new clue?" Zoe pointed to the gold envelope in my hand.

"I don't know. I haven't had time to look. Too busy breaking sprinklers and traveling to Holland."

"You mean, the *Netherlands*." Zoe chuckled. "Open it up. Maybe we'll get some guidance."

I opened the flap and pulled out a folded paper with the number two on it.

Zoe pulled some of the blanket back her way. "This is kind of fun."

"Yeah, except I keep wondering when Mr. B's gonna jump out of a bush and tackle me again. And I'm confused how I'm supposed to fix his windmill. I just know it's something I have to do. It's scary."

"Don't dwell on your fears. Read instead."

I unfolded it and read,

> ## Hole number seven: Where generosity goes, refreshment flows.

"Hmmm." Zoe lay back on her pillow and stared at the ceiling. "That's a great truth. But what's on hole seven?"

I closed my eyes tight and tried to remember the course. All I could think of was a run-down shack. But everything was run-down on that course. Just then, my phone buzzed in the pocket of my sweats and I jumped a little.

"Who's that?" Zoe sat up and frowned.

No one should be texting me at this hour.

I pulled my phone out and tried not to show a reaction as I read the screen.

> **Arcade, when you wake up, call me! I couldn't sleep, so I've been thinking of a way to help Mr. B. –Jacey.**

"Is it your secret admirer? Let me see." Zoe reached for the phone and I handed it over.

Let the teasing begin.

It must have been too late or something, because Zoe chose *not* to give me a hard time.

"Jacey's a nice girl. Hey, maybe she can help you with your windmill project . . ."

The windmill. Of course!

". . . but I still don't know why you'd want to help that mean old guy."

I reached up and grabbed the token around my neck. "Me either. I've always wanted to help people, but this is different."

"Because he's an enemy?"

"Yeah. It's not something that I would normally *want* to do. But in this case, after following the clues, and seeing that word 'Humility' on the windmill, I really believe I'm supposed to forget about how he's hurt me and do it anyway."

"Sounds like God is guiding you." Zoe pointed to my chest, where the Triple T Token lay right on top of my heart. "And he's using that token to do it."

"I guess. Why do you think that windmill has been broken for so long? How hard can it be to fix something like that? I mean, he's a business owner. He has money, right?"

Zoe shrugged. "Maybe it goes deeper than that. He did lose his wife, so maybe he's too sad to fix things. Or maybe he's trying to make some type of point. It could be a pride issue."

"Pride? How can he take pride in having a broken-down old mini-golf course?"

Zoe stretched out again. "People are complicated, Arcade. Who knows? I can't believe I'm saying this, but I'm starting to be like you, with more questions than answers."

"Hey, I have answers *sometimes*. That's why I read books. To find answers."

"Good luck finding an answer to *this* puzzle in a book." She pulled the covers off me, waking Loopy, and she turned over on her side. "Good night."

Loopy and I crawled over to the other half of the couch, turned off the lamp, and snuggled in. "Zoe, will you go to the bakery with me in the morning to talk to Jacey?"

"Of course. I have to keep an eye on you two lovebirds."

"ZOE, I do *not* like her!"

Zoe sat up and stared at me. "Seriously?"

"You know what I mean. I don't *like like* her."

"Yeah, right. Good night, Arcade."

"ZOE, I DO NOT LIKE LIKE HER."

Zoe flopped back down, folded the pillow over her ear, and sang, "GO-O-O-OD NIGHT."

CHAPTER 21

More Bread!

We need more bread," I said to Aunt Weeda first thing in the morning. "Can you drop me off at the Bridgeview Bakery on your way to work, please?"

"I would *love* to take my favorite nephew to the bakery." Aunt Weeda hummed a church song as she put together her lunch. For a woman who works as hard as she does, she's always cheerful. "Can you be ready in ten minutes?" She pulled money out of her wallet and handed me twenty bucks. "Spend all of this, now, you hear?"

"Thanks! It's just me and Zoe. Everyone else is still asleep."

"How will you get home?"

Hmmm. I hadn't thought of that. "It's only a couple of miles. We can walk. Virginia should look into getting some subways."

"You got that right! Okay, then." Aunt Weeda headed toward her bedroom. "I'll see you and Zoe in the car in ten minutes."

I crawled quietly onto the couch where Zoe was sleeping. I put my mouth right up to her ear.

"ZOE!"

She jumped, her arms flailing and her hair flopping around like a huge mop. I fell on my back on the couch, grabbed my stomach, and laughed as quietly as I could to keep from waking anyone else.

Zoe glared at me. "WHAT?"

"We're leaving for the bakery in ten minutes. Better wear one of Celeste's hats."

Jacey bounced over to greet us when we walked through the door of the Bridgeview Bakery. The place was so busy we had to squeeze over into a corner to talk.

"Business has been booming," Jacey said. "And my parents have always wanted to give back to the community, so they donate some of their earnings each month to a different charity. This month, they told me that *I* could pick the charity! Isn't that exciting?"

Jacey was wearing a bright yellow T-shirt that accentuated her cheerfulness.

She went on. "I've been reading in the Bible how Jesus said that when we give, our left hand shouldn't know what our right hand is doing."

"Huh? How can *that* work?" I held out both hands, then put one behind my back and laughed.

"What he means is," Zoe added, "it's best if we do things not expecting credit or reward."

"YES!" Jacey made me jump. "And that's where YOU come in, Arcade! You just happened to call me for a ride home from Forest Games and Golf right when I was thinking of who I could help! That's no coincidence! I know I'm supposed to be helping Mr. B. And since you're one of the nicest people I've ever met, I thought maybe you'd want to be in on it. I mean, while you're still here in Virginia. Because I don't think that's a coincidence, either. How long are you staying?"

"About a month."

But the token may have other ideas.

"PERFECT!" Jacey's eyes widened, and so did her smile. I wondered if she'd already consumed a dozen or so donuts to have this kind of energy in the morning.

A small table opened up right next to us, so Zoe led us over. "Tell her your idea about the windmill, Arcade." Zoe leaned back in her chair and gave me a stupid grin.

I shot her an *I don't like her, Zoe!* look.

Jacey took a seat and leaned in. "The windmill? Tell me!"

My token heated up a bit, and I glanced over at the bridge mural on the wall. "I was thinking that maybe I could help Mr. B get his windmill fixed and set it upright again. But I wanted to do it without him knowing it was me."

"Anonymously." Jacey grinned and nodded.

"Yeah. That's the only way it would work for me."

No joke.

"That's a FANTASTIC idea! Let's do it! Do you think Celeste, Derek, and your friend Doug would want in on it too?"

"Oh, they're *all* in."

"Great! I wonder where we should start? We would need some paint and tools—"

"And a small crane to lift it up." I wished my mechanically inclined friend Scratchy were here. He'd have that thing back up and running in no time.

"Hmmm." Jacey leaned her head on her hand. "I feel like I need to go and look at it more closely before we formulate a plan. But we can't just go sneaking around in there without looking suspicious."

"How about we go play a round of golf today?"

Jacey grimaced. "I told my mom I'd help her out all day."

"How about tonight? We could go after dinner. I think it's Glow Golf night."

Now Zoe was leaning in, smiling.

Stop. It. I glanced at my sister.

Jacey jumped up. "Let me go and ask my mom. I'll be right back!"

She jetted behind the counter, answering a few customer questions along the way.

I glared at Zoe. "I know what you're thinking, and I'd rather you not speak right now."

She just wiggled her eyebrows up and down.

Jacey was back in a flash. "Mom said it's a great idea. And she said she'd drive us! Can we pick you up at eight thirty?"

"Sure. Let's do it."

"Awesome! It's a date!"

Gulp. *A . . . DATE!*

"Jacey! Can you come in here and pull the bread out when it's done? I have to make a delivery in a few minutes." Mrs. Green wiped her floury hands on her apron as she approached our table. "Great to see you again, Arcade and Zoe. Did you come for more cinnamon bread?"

I held out the twenty-dollar bill. "You bet. And a few other things. My aunt ordered me to spend the whole thing."

"That was kind of her." Mrs. Green smiled and called back to a worker behind the counter. "Victor, make sure you throw in a few extra donuts for these kids, okay?"

"Gotcha, Mrs. Green!"

"Okay, then. I guess I'll see you kids tonight." Mrs. Green headed back to the kitchen.

Jacey stood. "See ya tonight!" Then she took off.

Zoe smacked me in the forearm. "Yep. It's a date."

CHAPTER 22

Glow Golf

The rest of the day dragged along as we worked to clean up the backyard. Doug mowed like a madman. And, because the water was turned off this time, Derek and I were able to fix three broken sprinkler heads. Zoe and Celeste talked and talked while they pulled weeds, and they even planted a few flowers in the pots on Aunt Weeda's patio. It would have been great to hang out there all night, watching the sun go down and drinking cold lemonade.

But I had a date. No, *we all* had a date! To figure out how to fix a windmill.

"How many rounds?" The teen boy behind the counter asked. His smile grew as he looked around me. "Jacey? What's up? Aren't you out a little late for a bakery girl?"

"Hey, Jackson! These are my friends Arcade, Zoe, Derek, Celeste, and Doug. And Mom said I could sleep in tomorrow."

"Okay, then. Playing some glow golf, huh? That's what I'm talkin' about!" He turned to me. "How many rounds?"

"Uh, six."

"That'll be forty-eight dollars." Jackson got out some scorecards while I tried to process that huge bill. "Uh . . ." I fished in my wallet for some money.

Thankfully, Celeste threw a fifty-dollar bill on the counter. "Mom said it's on her tonight."

Thank God for Aunt Weeda. We'll have to make sure to get her money's worth.

Jackson took the bill and made change, which he handed back to Celeste. "Golf balls and clubs are right behind you. Only five people on a hole at one time, so you'll have to break up into two groups. Which course you playin'?"

"The windmill course," I said.

"Broken-down old windmill course. Everyone's favorite. You may have to wait a little."

"That's okay." Jacey took in a deep breath. "It's a nice night. We'll enjoy looking at the lights."

"Say hi to your brother for me, okay?

"Sure will. Hey, Jackson?"

"Yeah?"

"Does Mr. B ever go on vacation? Have a day off? He looks real tired lately. I'm worried about him."

"Hmmm. Let me check the schedule." Jackson poked some keys on a small laptop that sat on the kiosk. "Looks like he's gonna be out next Tuesday through Friday. Don't know why though. Want me to ask him?" He looked around, like he was going to bring Mr. B over here . . . where *we* were.

Nooooo!

"I don't see him or his vehicle anywhere. I think he left for the night."

Jacey smiled. "That's okay. You don't need to mention it. I'll talk to him this weekend when I bring his bread."

"You're the best, Jacey!"

We collected our equipment and headed out to the first hole. Laser and black lights illuminated the place. Even the golf balls had lights in them. Mine was gold.

I gathered everyone in a huddle. "Here's the plan. When it's your turn, walk up to the windmill, like you're planning your shot. Take some pictures and log notes in your phone, or just keep a mental list of the things we need to do to repair that windmill. And keep an eye out for video cameras."

"I haven't seen too many around here," Zoe said.

"Okay, then, here we gooooooo!" I laughed, remembering the famous quote from my sixth-grade teacher, Mr. Dooley.

We broke up into two groups. Celeste, Derek, and Doug went first. Zoe, Jacey, and I hung back.

"I gotta be your chaperone," Zoe whispered, and she hit me in the ribs with her elbow.

I handed her my club. "I was thinking you would make the perfect caddy."

When it was my turn, I walked up to the windmill and took pictures from every angle. The paint was chipped, and the wood definitely needed patching where it was laying in the creek. The sails looked okay—surprisingly—but there was no way to know if the spinning mechanism would work once we got it set up. What did Stephan call that? The sail frame?

"Hey! If you don't hurry up, we're going to need to play through," a couple of college-aged boys called to me from the bench at hole one.

I picked up my ball. "All clear!" I trotted down the hill to where Zoe and Jacey were taking turns putting their balls into the hole.

"Let's go cut in front of Celeste's group. I want to get to hole seven."

Zoe nodded. "Oh, yeah. Generosity. Can't wait to see what that's all about."

"Hole seven?" Jacey looked intrigued. "The one with the little house with the treasure inside?"

"Treasure inside?"

"Follow me. I'll show you."

CHAPTER 23

Go Golf

We played holes two through six, to get our money's worth. Celeste and Doug had a friendly competition going on. The one with the most strokes had to buy the other a slice of pizza. By the time they reached the green at hole six, Doug was losing by five strokes.

"Dude, the light inside this red ball is throwing me off. It's blinding me so I can't putt!"

"Would you like to trade colors?" Celeste handed Doug her purple golf ball.

"Yeah. I'm thinking purple is lucky." He placed it on the green and proceeded to take five more putts to get it in.

"Okay, I'll have my red one back."

"Check this out." Zoe opened her scorecard. "This golf course has *rules*! And it says you have to pick your ball up after *six* strokes."

Doug took his pencil and started erasing. "Cool! That means I get to erase all my tens? Celeste, you're going down!"

"There's a lot of rules to mini-golf. Who knew? Hey— check this one out!" Zoe began to read from the card.

"Be careful and watch your step as you journey near windmills, through villages, over bridges, and around waterfalls."

"Ooooh." I pretended to shiver. "Thanks for the warning." I set my gold golf ball down on the mat leading into hole seven. "Just what I thought, it's a plain little village house. It could use a paint job too." I hit the ball. It rolled right down the center of the mat and in through the door of the house. I held my club up in the air. "Oh, yeah! Right there, baby!"

Jacey took her turn after me, and her ball rolled into the house too. "There's a window in the back. Jackson told my brother about it, and he showed me once. Come on." I followed her down the path, around the house, and I shined my phone flashlight inside. Something rectangular and white sat on the ground inside the little house.

"It looks like some kind of fancy tray."

"Exactly," Jacey said. "It's a marble serving tray. From India."

"What's it doing in there?"

Jacey shrugged. "I have no idea. Seems like a waste of something so beautiful."

I pulled my head back, and the light on my phone fell on another gold plaque bolted to the back of the house. It said "Generosity." At the bottom, just like on the windmill plaque, was printed *Arcade Adventures*.

"Where generosity goes, refreshment flows. Huh."

"What?" Jacey bent down to check out the plaque too. "I've never noticed that before." She ran her fingers over the words. "Generosity. I like it!"

Right then, the token began to pulse light.

Oh, no! This is NOT the time!

Heat built up so high in my shirt that I had to pull the token out so I wouldn't get a blister. Jacey's eyes grew wide as she fixed them on the token. "That's cool! Did you get that here at the arcade?"

"Sort of. It's a long, crazy story."

"I like crazy stories."

Gold glitter began to fall from the sky. The laser lights hit the thousands of golden flecks, sending multi-colored flashes in every direction.

Oh, you're about to see crazy. Any second. I hope your mom won't mind.

Next thing I knew, Zoe was by my side. "Remember *me*, your caddy? I'm going to make a suggestion, Mr. Pro Golfer. Choose UP or DOWN this time."

"I'll consider it."

The elevator doors appeared, like they always did when the glitter fell. But this time, they were plain and attached to the back of the little house. Celeste, Doug, and Derek arrived, the pulsing light from my token and the golden coin slot flashing in their eyes.

"We doin' this again?" Derek asked. "Awesome!"

"Doing what?" Jacey backed up and covered her mouth with her hands.

Zoe patted Jacey on the shoulder. "We never quite

know for sure. Just stay close. Things are about to get . . . unpredictable."

I pulled the token off the chain and dropped it in the slot. The little run-down village house shined gold, and the doors opened.

"Should we check it out?" I stepped toward the open doors.

My friends all ran past me into the elevator! Jacey hesitated for a second.

"I . . . I . . . can't," she stammered as she slowly stepped backward. "My mom will be here at ten thirty to pick us up."

"We should be back immediately," Zoe said. "I know that doesn't make sense . . ."

"I've been through this before—lots of times—and it's always an exciting adventure. Come on, I'll have you back in time." I jumped into the elevator and waved Jacey in.

"Well . . ." Jacey looked around, and then back at me. "As long as I'm going with you . . ."

Zoe reached out and grabbed Jacey's hand, pulling her in.

I crossed my arms, leaned against the wall of the elevator, and smiled. "I'm glad you decided to join us."

"Me too." Jacey grinned, but I could tell she was still a little nervous.

And then the doors closed.

"LEFT or RIGHT?"

It was still my voice, but now it was a DIFFERENT choice. And, as usual, only one button.

"OH, PLEASE!!!!" Zoe paced around, shaking her head. "I finally got him to agree to pick UP or DOWN!"

"Hey! I didn't agree to anything, I just said I'd *consider* it."

"*Low* was fun, Arcade," Derek said. "How about *high* this time?"

"NOOOOOOO!" Doug whined. "And I wouldn't suggest *back*, either."

"Hmmmm." Celeste had her hand on her chin. "Arcade, are you right- or left-handed?"

"I'm ambidextrous."

"You are not!" Zoe threw her hands up. "Make a choice, Arcade. I know you won't listen to me, so how about you go with your gut?"

Go with my gut? My gut is churning around and around.

I stepped forward and pressed the button. "Around!"

"Hold on, everyone!" Zoe shouted.

I immediately regretted that decision. The elevator became like a washing machine, turning around and around. Thankfully, it spun so fast, the force plastered us to the walls instead of shaking us around. It was only when it stopped that we thumped.

The doors open, and a crowd of people are there to greet us!

"Namaste!" they call to us, holding their palms together and smiling.

One of the women, dark-skinned and wrapped from head to toe in colorful fabric, steps forward. "I am Neena. Please, come." She points down a dirt road. "We are about to begin, and we would like to greet you in our traditional way."

We follow the friendly bunch into a simple meeting hall. Several rows of metal chairs are filled with people who are dressed in bright reds, oranges, yellows, and greens. A banner hangs on the front wall that says:

MID-INDIA YOUTH MISSION WELCOMES OUR GUESTS:
ARCADE LIVINGSTON, ZOE LIVINGSTON, DEREK CLARK,
CELESTE CLARK, DOUG BAKER, AND JACEY GREEN

Doug leans over and whispers through his smile, "Did you text them to let them know we were coming?"

"No, Doug! Only the token knows where we're going."

He nods. "Oh. So we're in India?"

"That's what the sign says. All the way *around* the other side of the earth."

The woman guides us up to the front of the hall. "Come here, please. We have saved you seats."

Sure enough, there are six seats. We walk up in a line and sit down.

The woman smiles at the crowd and talks in a different language. Zoe leans over. "That's Hindi."

"Come," the woman points. "Stand in front."

She is so happy and inviting, we don't dare say no . . . or run out of the room. Instead, we go up, just as she suggests.

The woman talks some more in Hindi. I can only nod and smile. Then she turns to us and says, "Our friends have come all the way from Virginia to bring encouragement. Please welcome them."

How does she know we're from Virginia?

The audience claps. Then the whole back row of about fifteen men and women come toward us carrying necklaces made of orange and yellow marigolds. I'm thinking they will put only one on each of our necks. Instead, they pile on four or five! The last woman to place one around my neck points to my chain where the token hung before I placed it in the slot. She speaks in English with a heavy accent, "That is special to you."

Yes, it is.

Then she puts her palms together and dips her chin. "Namaste."

Zoe pokes me in the side. "That's an Indian greeting. Do it back to her."

I put my palms together. "Namaste."

Neena guides us back to our chairs, and then speaks to the crowd in Hindi again. Everyone stands and begins singing! They read words off an overhead screen. The Hindi letters loop together in a way that looks more like art than writing.

We can't read or speak anything, but everyone is clapping, and we know how to do that. It's a joyful few minutes.

We take our seats, and Neena points for me to come up to the podium.

Oh, please, not me.

I put my thumb to my chest and she nods. "Yes. You. Arcade. Please come."

"Oh, Lord . . . help him," Zoe says as I pass by her.

Neena speaks to me quietly at the podium. "These people work for our mission organization. Their jobs are teaching children, caring for the sick, and visiting villages to find out where help is needed. It is difficult work."

I scan the crowd. "Oh, wow. I like helping people too."

"I know." She speaks to the audience in Hindi and translates for me. "Arcade would now like to bring you a word of encouragement for your day."

Gulp!

She looks at me. "Go ahead. I will translate."

DOUBLE GULP!

The ten pounds of marigolds pull my shoulders toward

the ground. My hands shake and my forehead begins to drip. It's much hotter here than in Virginia!

"Ummmm . . ."

The woman says a few words in Hindi, and the people smile.

Thoughts swirl in my head.

You can do this, Arcade. You have people speaking encouragement to you all the time. Just say something!

I say a little prayer, and then I open my mouth. I have no idea what is going to come out.

"As you go out to help people today . . ."

Neena translates with a few long sentences.

"Remember to guard your heart. It determines the course of your life."

Good one, Arcade. You can never go wrong with Proverbs.

The people nod and smile as Neena translates, which buys me time to think of what to say next. I shove my clammy hands into my pockets, and I feel it. The golden envelope with the clues.

Of course. The clues!

Neena finishes up her translation, and I continue. "Because the journey starts with a humble heart." I glance over at Zoe, who looks like she's sitting on pins and needles. "Putting others ahead of ourselves brings joy to everyone."

Whoa! Where did that line come from? It's an Arcade original!

Neena translates and the crowd leans forward.

Oh, boy, I think they want more!

Neena glances over at me. I guess they want more. I clear my throat.

"And where generosity goes, refreshment flows."

That one takes Neena a long time to translate. Which is a good thing. Because it's all I've got.

I put my palms together and dip my chin. "Thank you. Namaste."

The people smile and clap. I can't believe what I've just done. I look over at Zoe. Her chin is on the floor. I drag my marigold-draped self back to the chair and plunk down.

Whew!

Neena continues to talk with the crowd in Hindi. And then it appears that she is leading them in a prayer. I bow my head and close my eyes.

Whatever they are asking for, please give it to them, Lord. They seem like such kind and giving people.

When Neena is done praying, she brings our whole group to the front of the stage, and EVERYONE in the room comes over to greet us again. Some shake our hands, some grab our shoulders and squeeze, some kiss us on the cheeks. That's a lot of hospitality for people they don't even know!

"Thank you . . . thank you . . . bless you . . . thank you . . ."

The greetings take longer than the whole meeting did.

"Man, they really like us!" Doug says. "No one ever treated me this nice before!"

I have to admit, I'm kind of overwhelmed with the greetings myself.

"Namaste . . . Namaste . . . Namaste . . ." My head is getting tired of bobbing up and down, and my neck is hot from the stack of marigold necklaces.

Finally, the last person departs, and I'm kind of sad. The room feels like all the joy got sucked out of it.

Neena approaches us, smiling. "Thank you for your encouraging words, Arcade. We would like to take you to visit a family that is suffering right now after the loss of their daughter."

"Loss? What do you mean?"

"She was sick for most of her life. Last week she passed away."

Zoe's eyes fill with tears. "But do you think the family will want us there?"

"Oh, yes, they would love to have you come. They live just across the road. Please, follow me."

We walk past a couple of modest buildings before passing some ladies who are hanging colorful clothes out to dry on a line. They smile and wave. We wave back. A thin cow wanders by. He's followed by a chicken.

India is AMAZING!

We continue along the dusty road until we come to a white fence surrounding a little yard in front of a small house.

I turn to look at Zoe and neither of us have to say a thing.

It looks just like the house on hole seven of the windmill course!

I wish Neena wouldn't walk so fast to the front door. My heart pounds.

What in the world will we say to this family to encourage them? The token must have made a mistake on this one. We're just a bunch of kids from Virginia.

"Good morning. Namaste," says the man who opens the door of the little house. He is holding a shiny-faced little girl with bright black eyes and black curly hair. She is smiling, happily chewing on a cookie.

"Namaste, Sanjay," says Neena.

Sanjay opens the door wide, inviting us into the living room. We squeeze past him and take seats on the small couch and a plastic chair set up in the room. He shouts some Hindi words toward the back of the house, and a woman in a green wrap enters. She hugs Neena, and then reaches out to each one of us to shake our hands.

"Sanjay and Grace, this is Zoe, Celeste, Derek, Jacey, and Doug. And this young man is Arcade."

Why did you announce me separately? And why do I get my own chair in the corner when everyone else has to share a space on the couch?

Grace disappears, and I wonder if her sadness mixed with our intrusion is too much for her.

"We can come back later," I say to Sanjay. He holds up a finger and disappears, leaving the happy little girl in our company. She looks over our group and begins to giggle.

"You are sooooo cute!" Celeste goes over to the little girl and swoops her up. "You have the most beautiful eyes I have ever seen!" She rocks her back and forth, and the girl offers her a bite of her cookie. When Celeste opens her mouth to take a bite, the girl pulls it back.

"Ha! She got you!" Derek slaps his knee. Celeste gives him a glare, but then looks back at the little girl and laughs.

"I think you've met your match," Zoe says.

"Can I take you back to Virginia with me?" Celeste hugs her tight and swings her around the tiny room.

Soon, Sanjay and Grace reappear. Grace is holding a tray with bottled water and packaged cookies. "Please." She holds the tray out to me. "Have some refreshment."

Refreshment?

I take a water bottle and cookies. When I do, I notice that the tray is white, with other colors inlaid.

Marble from India!

Grace moves around the room with the serving tray. When everyone has something, she walks back out of the room and returns with another full tray! She sits down next to her husband. The little girl sits on Celeste's lap and plays peek-a-boo with her.

Sanjay speaks in English. "Thank you for coming."

"We are sorry about your loss," Zoe says. She can barely look him in the eyes.

"Yes. We are very sorry," Doug says. I notice he has not taken any cookies, just water. "Is there anything we can do for you?"

"It means a lot to us that you have come to sit and visit." Grace reaches up with her scarf and catches a tear dripping off her chin. She looks over at the little girl. "Shiny likes you," she says to Celeste.

"Shiny! That's a perfect name for her."

"That is what we thought when we saw her for the first time." Sanjay waves at his little daughter.

"What is it like in . . . Virginia?" Grace asks. "I have never been there."

She sits back and listens intently as each one of us tells her about our favorite things in Virginia. There is gentle laughter, especially when Derek tells about how green the landscape is when you water it correctly. And when you avoid breaking off sprinkler heads, causing visors to fly and yards to flood.

Jacey explains about how she and her family own a bakery. "One time a lady from India came and taught me how to make naan."

"Naan?" I don't have a clue what that is.

The comment sends Grace back to her kitchen, and she returns with the marble tray filled with a basket of tasty flatbread.

"Oh, yeah. Naan is the bomb!" Doug grabs two pieces and downs them in seconds.

"Do you have animals?" Neena asks. She seems in no hurry, simply at peace enjoying the conversation with new friends from around the globe. I feel the exact same way.

"I have a dog named Loopy," I answer.

Shiny laughs and tries to say it. "Ooopy."

"Yes! He's a little chocolate-colored furball. And he slobbers a lot. I'm sorry he's not here."

"Ooooooopy!"

Grace and Sanjay laugh.

Something tells me this little girl is going to bring joy to lots of people in her life.

An hour or so goes by. We have eaten through two serving trays of cookies and two baskets of naan before Neena finally stands. "We would like to pray with you before we go." We form a circle and bow our heads. "Arcade, would you be so kind to say the prayer?"

My heart pounds. This isn't like earlier in the meeting. I can't use others' words for this! This has to come from the heart. I wait a second, and then open my mouth.

"Dear God, thank you for our new friends, Sanjay, Grace, and little Shiny. Please comfort them during this difficult time and bring them joy in the days and weeks to come. Keep them healthy and filled with hope. And bless them for their generosity. Amen."

For a few moments, there is only silence, except for sniffling coming from our whole Virginia crew. I'm afraid to look up. When I do, I see Grace and Sanjay smiling at each other. And then Shiny yells, "OOOOOOOOOOOPY!" and it makes everyone laugh.

Neena leads us to the door to leave, and Grace puts her hands out to stop us. "One moment, please." She disappears again and comes back . . . with gifts!

"Oh, no, we couldn't . . ." A tear rolls down Zoe's cheek.

"You must," Neena says. "It brings them great joy to give."

Grace unrolls the balls of fabric she has carried in, which turn into scarves, each one a different color. She speaks to each one of us personally and explains why she picked specific colors for each of us.

"Zoe is pink, for beauty and love. Celeste, red, for strength and dignity. Green for Derek, so that he will have luck with the sprinklers and the grass in Virginia. Brown for Doug, the color of naan, and orange for Jacey, one of the colors in a beautiful sunset." Grace then wraps a gold scarf around my neck. "Because of your heart. Thank you for visiting us today, Arcade."

I am at a loss for words. I've never experienced such hospitality and generosity from people in my life.

"Thank you. It's been an honor," I manage to say, putting my palms together and nodding my head. "Namaste."

"OOOOOOOPY!"

We all laugh as Shiny and her parents escort us out and wave goodbye, grateful and smiling in spite of their sadness.

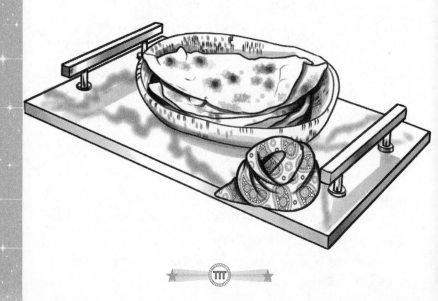

Neena is the fastest walker I've ever met. And I don't know if it's because it's so hot and humid, or if it's that we're so full of naan, but none of us can keep up with her. Another cow walks by, and then a chicken runs across the path, causing us to stop and fall further behind.

"Should we run?" Jacey asks. "I don't want to get lost in India."

Right as she says that, the Triple T Token returns to my chain. It shines through my shirt and lights up the gold scarf that is wrapped around my neck.

"I think we can stay right here." I feel the sprinkling of glitter on my shoulders. "Our elevator has arrived."

CHAPTER 25
Above and Beyond

The ride back to Virginia was peaceful—no bumping around.

"*Around* was a good choice." Zoe played with the pink scarf around her neck. "I wish we could have stayed longer."

Me too.

Soon, the doors opened and we stepped out behind the little village house at Forest Games and Golf. Laser lights flashed in the distance, and techno music blared over the loudspeaker.

"Who's up for hole eight?" Doug picked up his club and ran down the hill.

Jacey wrapped her orange scarf around her shoulders. "I feel a little silly playing mini-golf after our . . . experience."

I scanned the scenery. The windmill course looked so much better at night, when you couldn't really see the damage that had been ignored for so long.

Why hasn't Mr. B fixed the place up? He must have lost hope. That's the only explanation.

The token blazed heat. I reached up to touch it.

Or maybe he lost . . . this.

"Are you coming, Arcade?" Derek was now down the hill, along with Zoe, Celeste, and Doug. Jacey stood there with me, checking out the surroundings.

"Hey, Arcade. Are you thinking what I'm thinking?"

I cleared my throat. "Well . . . I was thinking that this whole place is a mess. How hard do you think it would be to fix it *all* up, not just the windmill?"

Jacey squealed. "That's EXACTLY what I was thinking! It would be hard to do it anonymously, but if we get Jackson and the other teen staff from Forest Games and Golf involved, it's possible. I don't know how we'll keep Mr. B away from here, but we'll figure it out."

"Hmmm. We might need a spy in a rocking chair."

"Huh?"

"Oh. Miss Gertrude. She lives at the end of Derek's street. I haven't talked to her in a while, but I think she might help us."

When we reached the break at hole ten, I gathered my team to talk about the possibility of fixing up the whole windmill course. "Take pictures of everything, and we'll make a list of what needs to be done tomorrow."

"Can we do that?" Zoe asked. "Do we have the resources?"

"Sanjay and Grace didn't have much. And they went above and beyond with their generosity. I think with all of us working together, we can do it."

"Operation ABOVE and BEYOND! I like the sound of that!" Jacey bounced up and down.

"We have to be careful, Arcade." Zoe gave me the concerned sister, furrowed-brow look. Then she pulled me aside, away from the crowd. "I was there when Mr. B tried to take the token from you! This guy is dangerous. How do we know that he's not just using the business as a front for some crime ring? What if we're just helping him succeed at doing something rotten?"

"You have a point, and this time it's not just on top of your head."

Zoe pushed me. "Hey, I'm just trying to protect you, fish face."

"Fish face? What kind of fish has a face like this?" I smiled and tilted my head to look like a model.

"Any fish that is lured by bait and then ends up with a hook in his mouth!"

"We'll be extra careful," I reassured her. "In fact, I was thinking about bringing in a grown-up to help us."

"A grown-up? If we tell Aunt Weeda, she'll just talk to Mom and Dad and then they'll make us go bac—"

I put my hands out. "Not Aunt Weeda. I was thinking about Miss Gertrude."

Zoe stopped and stared. "Ohhhhh." Then she grinned. "That could work."

CHAPTER 26

Miss Gertrude

Zoe and I went to see Miss Gertrude first thing in the morning. We snuck out of Derek's house while everyone was still sleeping, walked around the back of the houses, through the Cimarron woods, up the steps to her back door, and knocked.

Nothing happened.

"Do you think it's too early?" Zoe pulled out her phone to check the time.

"Nah. Older people are *always* up early. Maybe she didn't hear the knock. Try again."

Zoe knocked harder.

"I'm comin'! Don't leave!" Miss Gertrude's sweet voice rang through the door.

In a couple of minutes, she opened the door, wearing a multi-colored robe and bright pink slippers.

"Zoe and Arcade Livingston! I've been waiting for you!" She pushed open the screen and welcomed us in.

"You have?" The token on my chest jumped and plunked.

"Oh, yes! I've seen all you kids hiking out behind my

house the last couple of days, and I was hopin' you might stop by and say hello. Come, sit down, and tell me all about New York City."

How does she know we moved to New York?

She led us into her small living room that was filled with antiques and pink-flowered furniture. The place smelled like sweet soap. A furry orange cat jumped in my lap as soon as I sat down.

"Goldie, do you like Arcade? You always know good character, don't you?" Miss Gertrude sat down in a padded rocking chair that faced us and the large window in the front of her house.

I jolted when I looked outside. Her window looked right out at Mr. B's silver truck, sitting in his driveway across the street.

"Is everything all right, Arcade?" Miss Gertrude's eyes were focused on me. Then she looked down at my chest. The Triple T Token hung inside my shirt.

I cleared my throat. "Yes, I'm fine."

Might as well jump right into it.

"Miss Gertrude, do you know the man who moved in across the street?"

Miss Gertrude rocked a few times and looked out the window. "Do I know the man who moved in across the street?"

I suddenly felt like Doug was here.

"Do *you* know the man across the street?" Miss Gertrude had her hands clasped on her lap.

"Ummm. Not very well. What I do know is not good.

He's been following us, and he thinks I stole something from him."

Miss Gertrude leaned forward. "*Did* you steal something from him?"

"No, ma'am."

"Then why are you worried?"

"Because he thinks I did."

"Do you think you can prove to him otherwise?"

"Maybe. I . . . I mean, this doesn't make any sense, but my friends and I would like to help him fix up his golf course. Do you know Forest Games and Golf? We'd have to do it anonymously, though. Since he's after me and all."

Miss Gertrude rocked some more and watched out the window. "So you're trying to build a bridge to help restore the relationship?"

"Uh, I don't know. I guess so."

"Do you want me to help you?"

"Yes, please!"

"Would you like me to keep an eye on him? Keep him busy while you work?"

"That would be great. Do you think you can do that?"

"Do *you* think I can do that?"

I nodded. "I do."

Zoe, who had been giggling under her breath during the whole conversation, spoke up.

"Miss Gertrude, do you have a phone?"

Miss Gertrude tipped her head toward an old pink dial phone with a long cord hanging on the wall. "Does that count?"

Zoe got up and copied the number that was printed on the center of the dial. "Yes. But we won't be able to text you."

"Text? You mean write notes?"

And that gave me an idea. "Miss Gertrude, can we call you when we're planning to go to Forest Games and Golf? We can leave notes under your back doormat to keep you posted on what's going on too. We don't want Mr. B finding out we're partners."

Miss Gertrude laughed. "You think I can bend *all the way down* and look under my mat every morning?"

"We'll put them under the flowerpot on the little table instead," Zoe said. "Can you check it several times a day?"

Miss Gertrude nodded, got out of her rocking chair, and looked out the window. Mr. B had appeared and was walking across the street, toward her front door!

"Would you like me to start helping you right now?"

A jolt of adrenaline shot through me. "YES!"

Zoe and I ran toward the back door. Miss Gertrude called after us, "When you comin' back to tell me about New York City?"

"Soon!"

With our hearts racing, we sat on the back steps and scribbled down our phone numbers on a scrap of paper. We anchored it under the flowerpot and ran out into the Cimarron woods, not stopping until we plunked down on some lawn chairs in Derek's backyard.

"That was funny," Zoe slumped in the chair, huffing and puffing.

"WHAT was funny? You're crazy, girl! I didn't find ANYTHING funny about it."

Zoe gave me a smirk. "After Miss Gertrude sat down in her rocker, did you notice that she *only asked questions*?"

"No, she didn't! She told us she knew Mr. B and that she would help us."

"No, she *asked* us if we wanted her to help us."

"She said I had good character."

"No, she didn't! She *asked* Goldie."

"Really? She only asked questions? Wow! I like her. I'm glad she's on our side."

"Is she?"

"Is she what?"

Zoe pushed me over on the chair. "On our side?"

"She's an old lady! She's *not* a bad guy."

Zoe laughed. "I'm just messin' with you. But, remember, we can't trust everyone, Arcade. So be careful!"

Doug came out the back door. "There you are! You all want some bacon and eggs? We got some cookin' in the kitchen!"

CHAPTER 27

Building a Bridge

After downing a couple of pounds of bacon and finishing off all the baked goods in the house, we sat down around the table to make plans for Operation Above and Beyond.

"Let's see your pics," I said. We scrolled through everyone's phone and took notes. The damage seemed worse on the special features of the course, like the windmill and the little house, while most of the benches just needed a fresh coat of paint.

"That last hole is whack," Doug said. "The chain netting is broken so you can just walk up and throw your ball in to make a hole-in-one."

"I think I can fix the net," Derek said. "And we can all paint. The only tough job is getting that windmill set up. We need a crane for that. And there's that suspension bridge on hole twelve."

"Bridge? There's a bridge?" I scrolled through my pics and saw no bridge.

"Well, there used to be a bridge that went over the creek," Celeste said. "Now there's just poles on either side and some dangling chains. I remember jumping on it and calling it the 'bouncy bridge' when I was a kid." She scrolled through her pics. "I found this gold plaque on one of the poles. Check it out."

We all got up and gathered around Celeste. My jaw dropped when I read the word on the plaque.

Forgiveness.

And below it, just like on the other two plaques, it said *Arcade Adventures.*

"What's forgiveness got to do with a bridge?" Doug chewed the last crust of cinnamon bread.

"Arcade, didn't Miss Gertrude say something about building a bridge?" Zoe took out a notebook and began scribbling notes.

"Yeah! She asked if I wanted to build a bridge. Something about restoring a relationship, but I didn't get it. It's not like I had a relationship with Mr. B to restore."

"Yeah, I thought that was weird too."

I dug in my pocket and retrieved the golden envelope. "If there's a plaque, maybe there's another clue to go with it." I opened the envelope and pulled out another folded paper.

Hole number twelve: To truly live, you must forgive.

I scratched my head. "Can forgiveness build a bridge? Hmmm."

We all just sat there for a moment, and then my phone rang. It was Dad!

"I wonder why Dad's calling so early. Didn't he have to work late last night?"

Zoe shrugged. "You better answer it."

I pushed myself away from the table and ran into the living room. I flopped onto the couch. Zoe joined me. I put it on speaker.

"Hey, Dad! How come you're up?" My heart thumped and thumped in my chest.

"I had yesterday off. It sure is quiet without you and Zoe here."

"Isn't Milo keeping you company with his obnoxious bawking?" Zoe pinched me on my upper arm. "Ouch!"

"You okay, bud?"

"Yeah, I'm fine. How's Mom?"

"Mom's been busy. Hey, I have to tell you something. Lenwood Badger is out of jail."

"Lenwood?" I tried to sound calm, even though I already knew that since he was living right down the street.

"Yes. He's out on bail. Mom and I are making arrangements to bring you and Zoe back here, so we can keep a better eye on you."

"No!"

"What?"

Zoe grabbed my arm. "Hey, Dad, Zoe here."

"Oh, hi, sweetheart."

"Hey, Dad. We're totally safe here. We've all got each other's backs. I'd really like to stay if possible. I mean, how can that guy know that we're all the way in Virginia? And anyway, he was just a dumb suitcase thief."

"Good try, Zoe. I agree with you somewhat, but your mom won't. Anyway, I just wanted to give you a heads-up. We'll be in touch with Weeda and figure out the best time to fly you back here."

"Why don't you guys come *here*?" That was a surprise coming out of my mouth.

Zoe pinched me again.

"OW!"

There was silence on the other side of the phone. "Hmmmm. I'll give that some thought. I have a little break coming up, but not sure about Mom . . ."

"Plus, Doug really loves Virginia. We can't mess up his vacation."

"I think Doug loves being anywhere you guys are. I'll talk to Mom tonight though, and let you know what we've decided."

"Yes, sir. I do miss you and Mom."

"We miss you both too."

I hung up and Zoe sat there with her arms crossed. "Are you thinking what I'm thinking?"

"Speed up the process of getting the golf course fixed?"

Zoe held out a fist. "Let's do it!"

We ran back to the kitchen and shared the plan.

"We gotta tell Jacey!" I gathered my phone and the clues, and we all grabbed water bottles for the hike. We took off out the back of Derek's house, around the Cimarron woods, to the backyard at Miss Gertrude's. We scribbled a "text" on a piece of paper and entered the time and date on the top.

"This is kinda fun," Doug said. "Communication. Old-fashioned, like."

I wrote the note:

> *Project will take place sooner than planned.*
> *Stay tuned . . .*

I lifted the flowerpot and found a business card for a place called Darden Hoist & Crane. A note was scrawled at the top.

> *David Darden is a friend of mine. He will do*
> *the job for free. Call him.*

"Dude! Check this out! Miss Gertrude is the bomb!" I showed the card around.

"We'll call him when we get to the bakery," Zoe said. "Let's go."

Virginia could *really* use a subway. These two-mile runs were wearing me out!

The Virginia humidity wasn't too high, so I couldn't figure out why Derek, the basketball star, was falling behind. I held up so I could talk to him. He was looking at something on his phone screen.

"Whatcha readin', Derek?"

"I'm reading about how to fix that bridge. It's fascinating how suspension bridges work."

"You're kind of an engineer type, aren't you?"

"What do you mean?"

I stopped to walk a little. "You're interested in scientific design. Physics, geometry, that kind of stuff."

"Yeah, I guess you're right. It fascinates me."

"I wish you could meet Scratchy, my friend in New York. He loves fixin' things. You two would make short work of that bridge, I bet. He'd for sure have all the tools we would need."

"Yeah, my mom doesn't have a lot of tools."

"Maybe Miss Gertrude knows a tool guy."

"Miss Gertrude knows everyone. And everyone loves her. Well, except for Mr. B. I wonder why he doesn't like her?"

"Who knows? He's the one who's crazy. Hey, Derek, you think you'd want to go to the library after we hit the bakery? I bet they'll have a book on building suspension bridges."

Derek stopped to catch his breath. "The library's another two miles from the bakery, Arcade. How we gonna get there?"

"The bus? Or maybe we can help Mrs. Green on another delivery and she'll drop us off."

"HEY! SLOWPOKES! YOU TRYIN' TO DITCH US?" Celeste was now running backwards.

Derek shoved his phone in his back pocket. "I wish you would move back here, Arcade. Life sure picked up when you came back."

How am I gonna tell Derek that I have to go back early?

CHAPTER 28
Scones and Cranes

ey, Jacey! I'm glad you decided to come help your mom after all." I had texted her before we left to make sure she'd be at the bakery. I wouldn't have blamed her if she slept in after last night's adventure.

She smiled. "I'm an early bird. Can't help it."

"Do you have some time to . . . plan?" I looked around. There was a crowd, as usual. Jacey took off her apron and hung it on a hook on the wall. "Sure. I wasn't really scheduled today, so Mom has plenty of help. You want some blueberry scones?"

"Does anyone ever say no to that?" Doug asked.

Jacey laughed. "Never." She skipped toward the back and brought out a huge stack of scones. "Do you want to sit outside?" She took us out to some picnic tables on the side of the bakery that I had not noticed before. One happened to be open with a nice shade umbrella over it.

"I've been calculating costs," Jacey said, as we all sat down around the scones. "I think with the bakery money, we can provide the paint and hardware for the small repairs. I don't know if we'll have enough to rent a crane . . ."

I slid the business card in front of her. "Miss Gertrude knows a guy who will do it for free."

"WHAT?"

Whenever she does that, I jump. Can't help it.

"Wow—Arcade! See how God provides? This is FANTASTIC! Shall we give him a call?"

"Hold up," Zoe held her hands out. "First, we have to decide *when* we're going to do this. And it has to be soon. Arcade and I may be returning home earlier than expected."

"NO! Please, NO." Celeste crossed her arms and frowned.

"We're working on an extension," I said. "But just in case, we have to get this thing done fast."

Jacey's eyes lit up. "Jackson said that Mr. B would be gone next Tuesday through Friday. Should we start on Tuesday?"

"I don't see any other choice." I reached for a scone and broke it in half. "We also have to fix a bridge."

"A bridge?"

Celeste pulled the picture up on her phone. "This used to be a suspension bridge. See the cables?"

Jacey's eyes grew wide. "Oh. That's a mess! What do we need to fix that?"

"I'm gonna figure that out. Arcade and I are going to the library after this." Derek was looking more and more like an engineer than an NBA point guard lately. "But for now, I'm thinking we need some lumber and some suspension cables."

"Mmmmm. Sounds expensive," Jacey took a bite of a

scone and stared up at the puffy clouds. "But we're gonna do it. It'll all work out."

"I think I need to move to Virginia so I can eat at this bakery every day." Doug shoved a whole scone in his mouth.

Jacey laughed. "Hey, did you guys walk here? Would you like a ride to the library?"

"Girl, you just read my mind." Celeste rested her head on the picnic table.

We planned for a few more minutes, and then Jacey went to go ask her mom to give us a ride to the library. She came back with an older boy. "This is my brother, Jaden. He'll drive you to the library. And he's going to call his best friend, Jackson, at Forest Games and Golf and find out a little more about Mr. B's 'vacation' next week."

The young man jingled some keys and pointed to a bakery van in the parking lot. "You'll have to pile in there. I have some cakes to deliver to an office party. I think it's cool what you're doing for Mr. B."

"Jaden also knows where we can get some wood to fix the bridge! Isn't that great?"

Jaden dropped us off at the library before he delivered his cakes. It was nice to revisit the Forest Public Library. The regular librarian, Mrs. Chambers, wasn't there, but there was a guy named Patrick filling in. He took us right to the section we needed—books about suspension bridges.

"You ever been to the Golden Gate Bridge?" Patrick

asked. "Man, that's a trip! Sometimes the thing is shrouded in fog. Good thing they painted it orange."

"Wait. The Golden Gate Bridge is *orange*? Then why do they call it the *Golden* Gate?"

He plunked the books down on the table. "You can read all about it in here, my friend. But it's best to see it in person. You'll shake your head in disbelief." Patrick walked away, and each of us grabbed a book and started studying.

Derek pored over the book about how to build a suspension bridge. "This looks fairly simple. It's not like we're gonna have cars driving over it."

"Zoe and I are going to go look at some landscaping books," Celeste said. "Maybe we can plant some flowers for Mr. B to add some color to the windmill course."

While we were researching, I got a call from Jacey.

"Hey, Arcade! So, here's the scoop. Jackson says that he overheard Mr. B booking a flight to New York next Tuesday. He'll be out of the state! Jackson says we'll have to do the work at night, since Forest Games and Golf doesn't close until nine o'clock. Can you do that?"

Work at night? What will we tell Aunt Weeda?

"Yeah, we can do it."

"Great!" I could practically see Jacey's smile through the phone. "Jackson said he could get some of the employees to help with the project. They're tired of working at such a dump."

"That's DOPE!" Goosebumps rose on my arms and legs. "I guess we are really doin' this!"

My Triple T Token flashed for a second and sent a warm shot through my torso.

"Can you call the crane company?" Jacey asked. "Because that's probably what we'd want to do first. Get that windmill out of the creek. Then we can patch and paint . . ."

I pulled the card out of my pocket. "I'll do it right now."

For some reason, when I dialed the crane company, my heart started racing and my hands got clammy.

I guess this is really happening!

"Yeeeeelllllow! This is Dave at Darden Hoist and Crane. How can I help you?"

"Uh, hello. My name is Arcade. Miss Gertrude gave me your name as someone who might be able to help me pull a windmill out of a creek?"

"Arcade! Yeah! I remember you! How's it goin', man? Gertrude told me your plan. It's been a long time comin' for those brothers. Just tell me what time and when."

"Ummm, okay. Hey, thanks! I really appreciate it. Looks like we're scheduled for next Tuesday, right after they close. How about nine thirty?"

"I gotcha down on my schedule. I'll get in and out of there quick. Man, Forest Games and Golf. I remember when it was called Arcade Adventures. It was so much nicer back then. If only those brothers could have got along . . ."

Brothers? Who are these brothers he keeps talking about?

"Thank you for your . . . generosity, Mr. Darden."

"You can call me Dave! Say, how are your parents doin'? I went to school with Abram and Dottie, you know."

"No, I didn't know that. They're doing fine. Just busy, working their New York jobs and all."

"Well, you tell them I said hi, will ya? And I'll see you next Tuesday. Nine thirty, sharp!"

Well, *that* was easy! I turned to Derek, who was still studying books about bridges. "We got ourselves a crane. You think you can build a suspension bridge?"

Derek jumped to his feet. "Positive! I'm gonna practice with some Popsicle sticks at home."

Doug popped him on the back. "Tell you what. I'll eat the Popsicles for ya."

Derek laughed. "Couldn't do it without you, brother." Then he gave Doug a high-five.

Brothers? What brothers could Dave Darden be talking about?

We checked out ten books. They ranged in topics—everything from woodworking, painting outdoor furniture, metal repair, suspension bridge-building, and landscaping, to a couple of books about the history of the Golden Gate Bridge. Turns out it *is* orange! International orange, to be exact.

"Let's leave a note for Miss Gertrude." Zoe slowed as we returned to Cimarron Road through the backyard of Miss Gertrude's house. "We need to make sure she can keep an eye on Mr. B and let us know when he leaves on his trip."

"We'll meet you at the house." Celeste was getting tired and was in a hurry. Derek and Doug followed her, dragging along with their books.

Zoe and I sat down on the back steps. She pulled a little notepad out of her pocket and began scribbling.

"When you're finished, I need to add something."

Zoe handed me the notepad. "Go ahead."

I wrote a simple question:

> *Does Mr. B have a brother?*

Then I folded it and placed it under the flowerpot.

Zoe gave me a funny look. "Well? Are you going to tell me what you wrote?"

I looked around. "Yes, when we get back to the house. I feel like we need to get out of sight."

We ran through the trees behind the houses in the cul-de-sac.

Zoe stopped and breathed in deep. "I love these woods. They remind me of when I was little. I never thought things would change so much."

"Me either. Do you like *anything* about our new life, Zoe?"

We walked along, slower now. It was nice, just talking with my sister.

"Yes. I like my high school. I'm excited about all my classes. And I love how independent I feel when I'm taking the subway."

I nodded. "I like that too. Anything else?"

"Well, this doesn't make sense, but I like discovering all the new things. It's not comfortable, like here in Virginia, but it's exciting. I think I grow when I'm not in my comfort zone."

I stopped and looked at her. "Yeah, you seem a little taller. Or maybe that's just your hair sticking up."

"You know what I mean, lame brain." Zoe stuck her leg out to try to trip me, but I jumped over it.

"HA! Missed me!"

I started to run, and Zoe chased. We ran right into a cloud of gnats. Several of them ended up in my mouth.

"Gross!" Zoe swatted and ran faster but the gnats kept swarming her head. "That's the one thing I don't miss about these woods! Bugs!"

We ran faster, and the swarm lagged, but then we got tired and they caught up. "Almost there, Zoe! I'll open the screen door and you can dive in the house!"

We ran faster. Soon we could see Derek's house in the distance. We almost made it, when the gnats turned to glitter.

CHAPTER 29

Happy Birthday, Arcade

Zoe and I hit the ground, coughing and spitting.

"Ugh! Glitter! Pfffft!" Zoe wiped her mouth and shook the gold stuff off her hands.

"It's better than gnats!" I did a little bit of sputtering myself. The Triple T Token heated up, and I pulled it out from under my shirt. "Guess we're going somewhere uncomfortable. Prepare to grow a couple of inches."

We stood up and brushed dirt and glitter off our clothes. Derek's house was sooo close, I wanted to run in and grab everyone to join us. But the doors quickly appeared, and so did that coin slot. I didn't dare delay. I'd done that before and had been sorry.

"I'm glad you're here with me, Zoe. I know I tease you a lot, but I—"

She put her hand over her mouth. "Don't say anything nice to me right now. I want to be annoyed."

"You WANT to be annoyed? O . . . kay." I reached for the token and pulled it off the chain. "So . . . are you in agreement that I should drop the token into this coin slot?"

"DO IT ALREADY!

Zoe's screech startled me, and I dropped the token. It went right in. I made a parting motion with my hands, and the doors opened. Zoe stomped in.

"NOW or LATER?"

A new choice? This is getting even more interesting.

But in order to keep Zoe annoyed, I had to pick something else.

"I'd like to go back to THE BEGINNING." I stepped forward and pushed the red button.

We're in a hospital hallway. I know because it smells like hand sanitizer and cafeteria food all mixed together. People shuffle from room to room in light blue paper shoes, with matching paper caps pulled over their hair. I step to the right, and something hits me in the back of the ankle, taking out a chunk of skin.

"OUCH!"

"Excuse me, I'm sorry. I didn't see you there." It's a woman dressed in scrubs pushing an empty wheelchair. "Are you kids lost? Visiting hours are not till tonight."

"Oh, yes, we're lost."

Lost? That doesn't even begin to describe what we are.

The lady crosses her arms. "This is the nursery. The

waiting room is back there. We're packed today, so if you're not waiting for a baby to be born, I would suggest you go back down to the lobby and ask for directions. Follow those exit signs."

"Okay, thanks." Zoe smiles and turns back toward the waiting room.

The woman charges ahead with the wheelchair.

"Why are we going back this way?"

"Research," Zoe says. "You said you wanted to go back to the beginning. This is where beginnings happen, right?" Zoe walks down the long hallway toward the waiting room. The nurse was right, the place is packed! We scoot over to a corner by a window and look outside. There is snow on the ground.

"Excuse me, sir," Zoe turns to an older man who is wearing a T-shirt that says "I'm the Grandpa" on it. "Do you have the time and date? I think my phone is off."

"It's 11:35 am," the grandpa says, "and hopefully today is going to be my first grandchild's birthday. January twenty second!"

Hearing that date causes goosebumps to raise on my arms.

The hospital elevator doors across the hall open, and a nurse emerges pushing a very pregnant African American woman wearing a hospital gown in a wheelchair. Walking next to them is a handsome dude who's not wearing socks and who looks totally nervous.

"You got this, Dottie!" His words echo all the way down the hallway.

Zoe and I stand there, stunned. Zoe picks up a brochure from an end table and shows me the title. *Baby Blessings—Forest Community Hospital.*

"You know what I think?" Zoe gives me a silly grin.

The goosebumps spread down to my legs. "No, tell me."

"That was Mom and Dad, and they just headed down to the delivery room to give birth . . . to you." She pulls out some glitter from her pocket and throws it in my face. "Happy birthday, Arcade!"

So here we are, back at MY BEGINNING. But why? Suddenly, my stomach starts to growl. *Who am I? Doug?*

"Zoe, I'm hungry."

"Who are you? Doug? Come on . . ." Zoe grabs my elbow and pulls me out of the crowded waiting room and down the hall. She passes by the exit sign that should lead us to the lobby . . . and hopefully food.

"Where are you going? We're not supposed to be here."

"I'm well aware of that, Arcade. But your token brought us here on your birthday, and I want to find out why. If someone stops us, we'll just tell them we're lost again. That's normal in hospitals." We turn a corner. "There it is!" Zoe points to a sign that says "Labor and Delivery." Behind the sign are some double doors I'm pretty sure we can't go through without a security clearance.

"Can I help you, kids?" A nurse sits behind the station to the right of the doors. "Is your mom in here having a baby?"

Well, yeah, but . . .

"Uh, I think we're a little lost." Zoe folds her hands on the counter. "We were in the waiting room, and my brother got hungry . . . you know how kid brothers can be . . ."

"So you're looking for the cafeteria?" The nurse smiles. "You can follow the exit signs, or here . . . we just had maps made of our hospital."

Zoe reaches for the map. "Thank you so much." She opens it up and nudges me over to the side of the nurse's station while she reads it.

I look over her shoulder and point to the cafeteria on the map. "There it is. Let's go."

Zoe looks at me cross-eyed. "I know how to read a map, Einstein." Then she whispers, "I'm stalling."

I mouth the word "Oh," and wait.

Soon another nurse comes out of the double doors, holding a small manila envelope. She hands it to the nurse who gave us the map. "This is Dottie Livingston's jewelry. Can you please lock it in the safe? She didn't want to give up that necklace with the medallion on it. Man, people are attached to their stuff . . ."

The nurse at the station takes the envelope. She picks up the phone and dials. "Hi, Gertrude . . . yes . . . are you free to come and put some jewelry in the safe for me? Yes . . . thanks . . . I'm the only one at the desk . . . yes, we're packed today . . . must be a good day to be born!" She hangs up.

"Thanks for the map!" Zoe waves to the nurse.

"You are very welcome."

Zoe begins to walk slooooowwwwly down the hallway.

"Did you hear that name?" I speak quietly in Zoe's ear. "Gertrude? How many Gertrudes do we know, huh?"

"Shhhhhh. I'm waiting to see."

We shuffle along. And then we hear an elevator ding. Zoe turns, and leans her back against the wall, pretending to read the map. I follow her lead.

An old lady emerges from the elevator and approaches the nurse's station. I strain to hear the conversation.

"I'll take care of it," the old woman says, and she starts to walk in OUR DIRECTION.

"Stay cool," Zoe says. "There's a drinking fountain." She points down a few feet. "You're thirsty, right?"

"Well, actually, I'm hungry." Zoe pushes me over to the drinking fountain and we bend over to take drinks, just long enough for Gertrude—*our* Miss Gertrude—to pass us in the hall.

And then we follow her down a few doors, where she stops. We jump behind a rolling cart full of medical equipment and squint through the shelves to watch her next move. She takes a key out of her pocket and puts it in the door. But before she turns the knob, she opens the envelope, reaches in, and pulls out a gold chain. The arcade token on the end of the chain flickers light right toward us. And then Gertrude drops the chain in her pocket, opens the door, and disappears!

"She just *stole* Mom's token! Miss Gertrude has the token!" I'm yelling while whispering, if that's possible. Then I feel something drop on my chest.

Zoe points to it. "No, *you* have it. I don't know why or how, but you have it."

The ding of an elevator door rings in my ears. "Whoa, that's loud!"

"What's loud?" Zoe gives me a confused look.

"The elevator . . . I think it's calling me."

"But the elevator is back there—"

"No, it's not."

The elevator is now between where we are standing and where Miss Gertrude ripped off Mom's token. And the flashing golden coin slot is right in front of it.

Zoe stomps her foot. "I don't want to leave yet! I was hoping to see a brand new, chubby-cheeked baby Arcade!"

"I guess we'll have to postpone the birthday party until later." I drop the token into the slot, the doors open, and we rush in.

We sit in the elevator and I freak out.

"Is Miss Gertrude a bad guy? I mean, she stole the token! Maybe she's in partnership with Mr. B! Maybe we should go get the note from the flowerpot and—"

Zoe stops me in the middle of my panic. "Maybe you should calm down just a minute. She mentioned your good character, remember?"

Thoughts swirl in my head. I remember her praying over me when I was a kid. Did she really mean that? Of course, she *had* to mean that! Now I know she was there the day I was born, and she took the token from my mom!

Why would she do that?

The elevator seems to take forever to return us to the Cimarron woods. It chugs, shakes, stops, and starts again. Maybe time travel is harder than traveling to other parts of the world. It sure is confusing, that's for sure.

Finally, it stops for good, and it dings real loud. The doors open.

And Celeste is waiting.

"Girl, those gnats are gonna to eat you alive! Get in the house!" Celeste pulled Zoe off the ground and flicked gnats out of her hair before bringing her through the back door. She totally ignored me.

"It's okay. I can brush off my own gnats." I followed them in.

Doug was already eating Popsicles, and Derek had a boatload of supplies scattered out on the kitchen table to make a model suspension bridge: string, cardboard, tape, scissors, a ruler, sandpaper, glue . . .

"This bridge is gonna be cool! You gotta eat twenty-four Popsicles, Doug, if we want enough sticks to build one deck. Thirty-six for two decks."

Doug slurped up the last bite of a grape Popsicle. "Why go for one deck when you can have two? Someone toss me another one." He looked over at me. "Arcade! You finally made it! You look a little hot! Wanna Popsicle?"

CHAPTER 30
Sneaky, Good Plans

Popsicle eating became an obsession over the next few days as Derek perfected his suspension bridge-building skills. He designed model after model, and we all got into it. The girls even painted the sticks with their unwanted nail polish.

Aunt Weeda was overjoyed. "You see? People complain about young people nowadays, always havin' their noses in technology. But look at all of you, being creative with wood and polish! I couldn't be prouder." Then she looked closer. "But you better not be gettin' any of that old nail polish on my kitchen table!"

Celeste grabbed some newspapers out of the living room and spread them out under the bridges. "We're doin' fine, Mama, don't you worry."

Aunt Weeda smiled. "You all gonna build me a new house someday?"

I laughed. "Sure! Just call us Livingston Clark Construction."

"What?" Derek shot out of his seat. "You mean *Clark* Livingston Construction, don't you?"

"Hey!" Doug swallowed a bite of Popsicle. "Don't forget Baker! *Baker* Clark Livingston Construction. After all, I suffered brain freeze for you!"

"Now, now," Aunt Weeda said, "I hear some pride settin' in to you, young men. Don't you *ever* let that happen. We all know that pride goeth before a fall."

"Pride *goeth* before a fall? *Goeth*?" I twisted up my face.

"Well, that's in an old Bible translation. But y'all know what it means. When pride creeps up in hearts, people fall. And kingdoms follow."

Hmmm. Windmills too?

Zoe and I kept Miss Gertrude informed of our plan by continuing to put notes under the flowerpot. I felt like we should talk to her in person, but I was a little scared after that trip to the hospital on the day I was born.

"Just trust," Zoe said. "Hopefully she's on our side."

After several meetings at the bakery with Jacey, we came up with a solid plan.

"Tuesday night is crane night," I reminded the group over a scone-snacking session at Bridgeview Bakery. "Getting the windmill up is going to be a huge project, so we need all hands on deck for that. Wednesday night will be wood patching, painting, landscaping, and fixing the steel net on hole eighteen. And on Thursday night, Derek and I will fix the bridge while everyone else finishes painting." I paused to look at the group, who were all staring intently back at me. "On Friday, Mr. B's employees will have a lot of explaining to do about why his windmill course looks so good."

On Sunday, after church, Derek and I ran over to Miss Gertrude's to add another note.

> *Please call me when you see Mr. B leaving for the airport.*
>
> *Sincerely,*
> *Arcade Livingston*

I left her a list of all our phone numbers just in case she couldn't get through to me. I've been known to lose my phone at important times.

I folded the note and lifted the plant to place it under the pot.

"Hey, what's that?" Derek reached under the pot and pulled out a card.

> ### Pattie's Paint Shop. Brilliant Color in Every Drop.

Under the business name, there was a note scrawled:

> *Pattie is a friend of mine. She will donate the paint.*
>
> > *Gert*

"Man, Miss Gertrude knows everyone in this town! She's the best!" Derek handed me the card, and I programmed the number in my phone.

"Says here she's closed on Sundays." I shoved the card in my back pocket. "I hope tomorrow isn't too late to call."

"Nah. Sounds like Miss Gertrude already got it squared away."

"I need to tell Jacey! That means there's money left over now to buy some more plants or something." I dialed Jacey. My cheeks heated up and my heart pounded.

You've called her before, Arcade. What's the biggie?

"Hello? Bridgeview Bakery. Is this Arcade?"

And now my ears were hot. "Hey, Jacey. I have good news."

"I LOVE good news!"

"Yeah, well, Miss Gertrude has a friend, Pattie, who's going to donate the paint."

"WHAT?"

I dropped the phone when she yelled, "WHAT?"

Then I kicked it around in the dirt for a few seconds before I was able to retrieve it and bring it back up to my ear.

I heard laughter in the background. "Did you drop your phone?"

"Um . . . yeeeeah."

"I do that ALL the time. Hey, I'm super busy with the bakery line right now, so let's talk later. I'm PUMPED about the paint. BYE!"

"Bye."

I hung up, and Derek was staring at me, grinning. "I see what's goin' on here. You like Jacey, don't you?"

"What? NO! Have you been talking to Zoe? I like her, but I don't *like like* her."

"Okay, yeah, you like her."

"STOP IT, Derek, or I will totally take you down."

"Only if you can catch me first!"

Derek took off toward the woods, and I chased after him. We used to do this all the time when I lived here. He knows I can't catch him since he's a basketball player, and he runs all the time. I used to come close sometimes, but now I live in New York City, and I don't run anywhere anymore. I just ride the subway.

I called Pattie's Paints the next morning.

"Pattie's Paints! Hope you are having a colorful morning! How can I help you?" The cheerful, sing-song greeting put me at ease right away.

"Good morning, this is Arcad—"

"Arcade Livingston? I am SO glad to hear your voice. I hear you need some paint! Just tell me how much, what colors, and when you need it. I'd do anything for you and your family. They've always been so generous. Your mom and dad helped me when my business was struggling a few years ago. We went to school together, you know. And I remember the day you were born!"

And now, so do I.

"Wow, thanks Miss Pattie. I'll have my friend Jacey call you back with the color list tonight, but we know we need it on Wednesday night to do some painting at Forest Games and Golf."

"That's what Gertrude said. Well, I say it's about time! What a shame about those brothers, right? Maybe this will help patch things up. Ha! Patch things up. Literally. I'm so glad to help."

Again, with the brothers? Why hasn't Miss Gertrude answered my question about that?

"Thanks so much, Miss Pattie. It might be a lot of paint. I hope that's okay."

"Oh, yes. I've seen the place. I'll have plenty for you. No problem."

CHAPTER 31

Raising Hopes and Windmills

Tuesday afternoon came, and I was excited and scared. The teen employees at Forest Games and Golf were prepared to meet us at nine thirty for a windmill raising. Dave, the crane guy, was gonna be there too.

Aunt Weeda got called to work on inventory all night in the retail warehouse till the end of the week. That was a prayer answered! And Jacey's brother, Jaden, was set to pick us up at 9:00 pm.

The only thing that hadn't happened yet was the call from Miss Gertrude. And the reason she hadn't called? The silver truck was still sitting in the driveway of 2292 Cimarron Road.

Doug and Derek had gone to check it out. "If he's leavin' today, it hasn't happened yet!" Derek wiped sweat from his forehead. "You think we should call Miss Gertrude?"

"You do it." I pointed to Zoe. "Please?"

Zoe rolled her eyes. "See how much you need me?"

She poked some numbers on the phone and pushed my forehead when I crowded in to listen.

"Hello? Miss Gertrude? This is Zoe . . . I'm fine . . . how are you?"

Oh, no! Has she forgotten about our plans?

"Yes . . . we were wondering about Mr. B . . . we see that his truck is still there . . ."

Zoe held the phone out so we could all hear.

"Oh, yes, honey . . . he's right here! I asked him to come on over and help me move some furniture . . . he's not too happy with me right now . . . I have some other jobs . . . What? Hang on a minute. He's calling me from the other room . . ."

"WHY is she doing that? She knows we need him to get out of town!"

Zoe put out a hand to calm me. "She knows, Arcade."

Miss Gertrude came back on the line. "Well, isn't that the funniest thing? He says he can't help me clean the fireplace because he has a flight to New York in two hours. He's leavin' right now."

Zoe sighed. "Thanks, Miss Gertrude." She hung up. "See, everything's under control."

So why don't I feel like it is?

Jaden picked us up at eight forty-five. He winked as he slid open the delivery van door. "Never hurts to be early, right?"

"Especially when we're talking donuts!" Doug jumped in the van first and climbed way in the back. My hands shook as I climbed in next. I grabbed onto the seat and slipped.

"Are you okay, Arcade?" Jacey had her hands over her mouth.

"Yeah, I'm fine. Just a little nervous, I guess."

"Me too! I'm so excited! I can't wait to see the windmill standing tall!"

"Yeah, just like the one in Holland," Doug said, but then covered his mouth.

"Some of our employees brought tools," Jaden said. "If we have to cut some of the rotted wood out of the windmill, we might as well do it tonight."

"Sounds good to me."

The ride to Forest Games and Golf seemed like seconds.

"We close in five minutes. We'll get the stragglers out so we can get this party started. And I'll show you where you can direct your crane guy."

Derek jostled me. "You have a crane guy, Arcade. That's dope!"

We all piled out of the van.

Crowds of smiling kids exited the arcade, some gnawing on the famous cardboard pizza, some holding stuffed prizes. If all went according to plan, by Friday this would be a brand-new place.

Dave Darden, the crane guy, even arrived early. "I've been wanting to raise that silly windmill forever. I offered to do it for free, but Kenwood would never let me. Stubborn old dog."

"Kenwood?"

As in "Kenwood? You rat"?

Mr. Darden smiled. "Yeah, he always hated that name. Has all the kids call him Mr. B."

I gulped. "I thought his name was Lenwood."

Mr. Darden grabbed his head. "Woohoo! Don't go getting those two confused. They wouldn't be too happy about that!"

Mr. Darden jumped up on his small, portable crane and drove it down the path the employees had marked out for him. We headed for the windmill, where a crowd of strong young men stood waiting.

"All right, boys, this won't take long at all. I'm gonna hook her up, and then lift her up. I need someone to direct me where to drop her down and then we'll fasten her into the ground."

Jackson helped Mr. Darden hook the top of the windmill up to his crane. Then he directed as Mr. Darden worked to lift the windmill up and out of the creek.

Cheers came from the crowd. It was great to see that thing standing!

It took about thirty minutes to get it in the right position and set down securely.

More cheers, laughter, and clapping.

Jaden came over to give me some great news. "They turned off the video cams. None of this will be recorded."

Whew. I hadn't even thought about the video cameras.

Soon the cheering stopped, and people went to work bolting the windmill to the ground and sawing off rotted wood pieces.

Dave Darden came over to shake my hand. "Congratulations, Arcade. You've succeeded in making something happen that would have been easy if people just learned how to forgive one another."

"Thanks. I don't think I really did anything."

"You brought a little hope to the situation. That's a big thing! And hey, now that the creek isn't obstructed, you can open the pipes and get that waterfall working again! The kids are gonna love it!" Mr. Darden jumped back in his crane and revved her up. "See ya, Arcade!"

I waved and watched him drive through the parking lot and disappear down the road.

Waterfall? What waterfall?

The first part of our project was finished by 1:00 am. The windmill course now had a working windmill!

Jaden had us home by one-thirty, and everyone fell into bed. All except me and Zoe. We stayed up for a special meeting on the living room couch. Loopy joined us. I put him on my lap and hugged him real tight. "Sorry we have to keep leaving you, boy."

"So how are you feeling about the project? Any problems so far?" Zoe had her pillow on her lap and was punching it a little.

"Just one tiny problem."

"What?"

"Mr. Darden referred to Mr. B as *Kenwood*, and when I said I thought his name was *Lenwood*, he told me not to get those two confused. But now *I'm* confused. Are there two Badger brothers? And if so, which one was in jail in

New York, which one just flew to New York, and the most important question is—"

"Are they both in New York now?" Zoe's eyes opened wide.

"Yeah. I really hope so."

CHAPTER 32

Patch and Paint

On Wednesday night, Jaden showed up thirty minutes early. "There's a buzz around town, Arcade. Everyone seems to know that the windmill is up. The local news called Forest Games and Golf and wants to come out and do a story."

"Oh, no! That's the last thing we want," Jacey said. "We want this to be anonymous. No interviews. No stories."

"It's okay, sis. Jackson told them they couldn't come till Mr. B returns."

"I wish we could have done the project all in one night, but the place is too messed up." My heart started thumping hard again, thinking that there may be *another* Mr. B lurking.

"Jaden, do you know if they can turn on the video cams just in the parking lot tonight?" Zoe fidgeted as she watched out the window, and I could tell that she was nervous too.

"I think so. Why do you ask?"

"Someone could monitor the cameras and give us a heads-up if a news crew comes by. Or anyone else who might be wanting to cause trouble for that matter. It is night, after all."

Jaden nodded. "Not a bad idea to have some security. I'll ask Jackson when we get there. In fact, I can watch the cameras."

Zoe sighed. "That would make me feel much better."

As we all poured out of the van, I hung back to talk to Zoe. "We need to stick together. Work on the same project. It's the token that they're after, so if we stay out of sight, everything should be okay."

Zoe moved in closer to me. "I got your back."

"I got yours too."

Zoe and I painted the back of the little village house together. I peeked in and smiled when I saw the little white marble tray sitting there. Fancy, yet not making a huge deal of itself.

"I wish we could go back and visit Sanjay and Grace. I hope they're doing okay." Zoe dipped her brush in a bucket of fresh brown paint and smoothed it on the side of the house.

"I know what you mean. I sure learned a lot from them about generosity." I looked over at all the kids who were painting and patching. "It's because of them that I got the idea to restore this whole place. Where generosity goes, refreshment flows."

"I guess your choice to go *around* wasn't so bad."

"You're admitting that out loud?"

Zoe put a finger to her lips. "Shhhh. That's not for everyone to hear."

We continued to paint, and I felt peace for the next little while. When I needed a break from flinging a paintbrush, I walked down the path and took a seat on a bench. I hadn't had time to read the last clue in the envelope yet, and this seemed like the perfect time to do it.

"ARCADE!" Jacey screamed at me from hole eight.

I jumped up and looked all around. My heart pounded out of my chest.

What is it now? And then a terrible thought crept in. *He's here. Lenwood Badger is here.*

"You just sat on WET PAINT!" A bunch of the kids laughed.

I turned and looked at the bench. There was a yellow body-shaped smear where I had been sitting. I breathed out hard and grabbed my chest. "Is *that* all?"

"Is that *all*?" Zoe had come down to meet me at the bench. "Isn't that enough?" Then she crumbled to the ground, laughing.

So I sat on her.

"Arcade! Get off! I don't want paint all over me!"

"Why not? You said you had my back. And there's paint on my back. So here you go! Did I ever tell you what a great sister you are?"

CHAPTER 33

Bridging the Gap

It was a relief to finally get to Thursday night. Our gang stayed home and out of sight all day, afraid we might run into townspeople who may ask us about what was going on at Forest Games and Golf. All we had left of the project were a few odds and ends—*and* we had to fix that bridge!

Derek had come up with the perfect design. It only took him five tries and ten boxes of Popsicles. Doug hadn't seemed to mind.

Nerves got the best of me. I just *had* to know what was going on at the end of the street. So I called Miss Gertrude.

"Hello? Who's calling?"

"Miss Gertrude? Hi. This is Arcade."

"Arcade Livingston? How are you doing, my friend?"

"I'm doing okay. Have you seen Mr. B?"

"Now why would I see Mr. B? Isn't he in New York?"

There she goes with the questions again!

"I don't know. I'm just a little nervous. We're so close to finishing the project, and I wouldn't want him to show up and spoil it all."

And take the token, and well, whatever else he might try to do.

"How does the windmill course look? Is it stunning?"

"Yeah, it really is. All we have to do now is fix the bridge."

"That's the only thing left?"

"And a few touch ups."

There was silence on the other end. I thought maybe I heard a sniffle.

"Miss Gertrude?"

"Yes?"

"Are you all right?"

"Do you trust me to warn you if they come back?"

"Yes. Yes, I do."

And then I was sure I heard sniffling. And a hang up! And now I was more nervous than ever.

THEY?

Jaden and Jacey showed up forty-five minutes early. Bakery people are prompt!

"Hope it's okay." Jacey giggled. "I could barely stand the wait."

Totally.

"Jackson called and said that the hardware and lumber you ordered has all been delivered," Jacey yelled back to Derek, who was sitting way in the back of the van. "They have it stored in the back of the arcade, and as soon as they close, a bunch of the employees are going to haul it over to the bridge area. Then you can work your magic!"

Derek sat up a few inches taller than normal. "I can't wait to get started!"

"Derek Clark—building bridges, baby!" I held up my hand to give Derek a high-five.

"So, Arcade, do you have any new assignments for the rest of us? Zoe and I finished planting last night."

Celeste had been the one to come up with the design for the flowers and plants, and she bossed everyone in just the right way the night before so that it got done and looked great.

"I think we should all stay by Derek and be ready to do whatever he needs. The bridge is the biggest project of the night, and it *has* to get finished."

"Roger that!" Doug yelled. "We got you, Derek!"

I smiled. It was fun to watch one of my new friends become friends with my old friend.

"Okay, here we goooooo!" Jaden pulled into the parking lot of Forest Games and Golf. He drove the van around to the back of the arcade. "I'm gonna go check with Jackson. Maybe he can close early or something."

We waited only a few minutes, and Jackson came running back, a huge grin on his face. "Everybody's gone! Jackson said they all started leaving about eight. Some buzz about being the last night of the renovations. We got ourselves a supportive community!"

Sure enough, the place was empty. Jackson put the "closed" sign up, and our work group showed up to haul the bridge materials.

It felt like Halloween to me. A little cool, exciting, *and* scary. My pulse increased every time I walked by a large tree or hedge.

Calm down, Arcade. He's in New York. Or they are.

Derek was the expert engineer on the job. He provided drawings for all of his workers, and he noted the tools and supplies needed for each step. It was fascinating to watch each board be placed, one step at a time, and no faster. When we were halfway done, Derek called a break.

"He needs pizza!" Doug ran into the arcade and brought out three large cardboard pizzas for us to share.

As I devoured my piece, I took a few minutes to walk the grounds and check out all the painting that was going on. Jacey had chosen the colors for all the benches, flowerpots, and signposts.

"The place looks great, Jacey. This was a cool project for you and your parents to help with."

"We couldn't have done it without you! I still can't believe how the timing worked out."

We walked together, and I breathed a little easier, knowing we were almost done. We even strolled over to the other golf course, the one that no one really plays.

"It's funny how all the bushes are trimmed, the fake grass is clean, and even the paint is bright over here. It looks like someone has been keeping this one up." Jacey shrugged. "I don't get that."

"Me either." I took a bite of pizza and surveyed the whole place. "It's all a big mystery, that's for sure."

"BREAK OVER! BRIDGE PEOPLE, REPORT BACK IMMEDIATELY!" Celeste had found the loudspeaker.

"Do you mind if I join you on the bridge project for a while?" Jacey trotted down the hill and over to the bridge with me. "My jobs are done for now."

"I'm sure Derek would love to have you on the project." I tried not to look at her.

I do not like like her.

"Great! I want to take a picture of your team when it's all finished."

"One plank left to go." Derek wiped sweat from his forehead with the back of his hand as he knelt on the latest installed board. The suspension cables held him, three-quarters across the widest part of the windmill course creek.

"You got this, Derek!" I was so excited for my cousin, the one who usually struggles at school. He sits on the sidelines there. But here, he was a skilled craftsman and bridge designer! If the NBA didn't work out, he could look into jobs in engineering or building.

Derek called out for a few more parts, and our team tossed them out to him and watched as he worked. At one point, he challenged me to come out onto the bridge. "It'll hold! Just hang on to the side chains."

"You sure?"

"Yes!"

"Go on out, Arcade! I'll take your picture." Jacey had her phone aimed.

So I scooted out, holding on tight to the chains. It was

a lot like the bouncy bridges I played on at the park when I was little. Only I didn't dare bounce this time, since it wasn't quite finished.

I came just a foot from Derek.

"Okay, stop there. I need to secure a couple more cables . . ."

And then my phone rang.

Who's calling me now? Everyone I know is here. Except Mom and Dad. And . . .

"Hello?" My breath became short and I prayed I wouldn't hear a certain voice at the other end.

"Arcade? This is Gertrude. I've been trying to reach you . . ."

I took the phone from my ear and looked at the screen.

Five voicemails? How did I miss that?

"Arcade, are you there?"

I grabbed on tight to the chain. "Yes, I'm here."

"Sweet pea, the brothers are home."

I knew exactly who she meant. Lenwood and Kenwood Badger. Two Mr. Bs! Double trouble. And just as that thought crossed my mind, two guys, who looked exactly alike, came from opposite sides of the course, shouting my name.

"ARCADE LIVINGSTON! YOU STAY RIGHT THERE!" The guy on the left, who looked like the one who tackled me in New York, was coming right for me.

"YOU LITTLE TRESPASSER!" The guy on the

right, who also looked like the tackler from New York, was coming at me from the other direction.

"Arcade!" Zoe grabbed the chains and began to cross the bridge.

"Zoe, I don't think it will hold all of us!"

"So what? We'll all fall in the creek and then they'll have a harder time catching us!"

Celeste came out next. "No, they'll have to *fight* us. And they'll be sorry."

"Mr. B! It's okay! Arcade is just trying to help!" I guess I should have filled Jacey in on some important details.

Next thing I knew, Jacey and Doug were on the bridge too. Four kids in front of me and bridge-builder Derek, behind. The rest of the crowd seemed frozen. I was so hot I thought my head was going to explode!

No, wait a minute . . . it's the token that is so hot it's going to explode!

I pulled it out from under my shirt. Two lasers flew out from it and hit both Badger brothers in the eyes, stopping them in their tracks.

"Should we jump?" Derek stood on the last board of the bridge, ready to do whatever I said.

I didn't have time to answer because suddenly all the laser lights in Forest Games and Golf turned on. Then glitter shot out until a huge cloud of it formed over the bridge. It dumped a few flakes on us kids, but it looked like a dump truck full fell on the Badger brothers.

Elevator doors appeared at the end of the bridge, and a pulsing coin slot beamed in my direction.

"Come on, everyone, follow me!"

I threw the token in and motioned for the doors to open. They did, and my friends and I crossed over the bridge into a LARGE, DARK elevator.

CHAPTER 34

Over

"U P or DOWN?" My voice echoed throughout what seemed more like a cave than an elevator.

"Arcade, where are you? I can't see anything! It's so foggy!"

I still had my phone in my hand, so I tried to start the flashlight app. Nothing. "I'm over here, Zoe!"

"Don't move, I'm following your voice." In seconds, Zoe poked me in the chin. "Oh, good, I found you."

"Is everyone here? Doug? Jacey?"

"Right here," the nervous voices echoed back.

"Me and Celeste are here too," Derek's voice rang out from across the cavern.

"UP or DOWN?" my annoying voice taunted.

A girl's hand touched my shoulder. It was Jacey. "I'm really scared, Arcade."

"It's gonna be okay. Just stay by me. I have to make a choice. Pray it's the right one."

"Okay."

I gripped my empty token chain with one hand and closed my eyes.

I don't want to go up or down. Or high or low. No more going around or back or even sideways. I just want all this to be . . .

I spied the small red light up ahead. I ran for it.

"OVER!" I hit the button as hard as I could.

I hear noises, like the doors are opening, but the fog remains. I smell sea air. Cold wind whips through my hair and chills me to the bone, even through my thick hoodie. The fog droplets coat my face. I can almost drink them.

"Brrrrr!" Zoe crowds in next to me and feels for my face. "Where have you taken us this time, Mr. Travel Guide?"

"I'm not the guide. It's the token."

"You've been the one choosing."

"Yeah, but it's been determining the destination."

"That makes no sense."

"And yet it does."

"Arcade," Jacey says in a little voice, "where are we?"

"I don't know. If only this fog would clear . . ." I reach out my hand and try to bat away the moisture droplets. As I do, the cloud that's been surrounding our heads moves. A ray of sunshine drifts in and illuminates our location.

"ARCAAAAAAAAAAAAADE? Are we on a BRIDGE?" Doug is behind me.

"DOUG, listen to ME!" It's Derek. "This is a *suspension* bridge, I can see the outline of the cables. We've been building them all week. You know it's safe. You can RELAX."

"It's okay, Dougie. I'm right here by you." Oh, good. Celeste won't let him fall into . . .

Wait a minute? What is under us?

It doesn't smell like sea for nothing. The sea rages below.

"Yo, Derek! You close by?"

"Yeah, Arcade, I can see you. Comin' over now." Derek is next to me in seconds.

"Dude," I whisper, "I don't want to freak Doug out, but I think we're on the Golden Gate Bridge. Am I right?"

Derek's face is dripping with moisture from the fog. "Yeah. I see one of the towers. It's the Golden Gate, all right."

I nod. "Okay, that's cool. We're tourists. We'll just gather everybody together and walk to the end. There's a nice welcome center on the San Francisco side. I read that in a library book."

Derek keeps looking around, turning his head left, then right. My glasses are now completely fogged over, so I hope he has a clue which direction it is to San Francisco.

"Which way should we walk, Derek? You're the bridge-master."

All of a sudden, the air clears, and blue sky and bright sunshine cause me to squint. Derek grabs my arm and digs his fingers in.

"Uh . . . Arcade?"

"Yeah, boss. What is it?"

"I don't think the welcome center's open yet."

"What do you mean, *yet*?"

"Well, before you can have a welcome center, you have to be ready to welcome guests."

"Yeah, and we're the guests!"

Derek shakes his head furiously. "Nuh-uh."

"What do you mean, 'Nuh-uh'? We're here, crossing the Golden Gate Bridge."

"Arcade, we're not crossing today. In fact, it's probably not gonna happen for a while."

Zoe taps my shoulder. "Arcade, take off your glasses and LOOK!"

I whip them off. My vision isn't great, but it's better without all the fog on the lenses. I stare up at the massive tower with the steel cables draping off both sides. Roadway extends beyond us for a few yards, but then I see . . . nothing.

"Tell me the road doesn't end there."

I wipe the water off my glasses with my sleeve, put them back on, and look in the opposite direction. My stomach does some major flips.

It's the same view the other way! The road extends for a while then ends. Neither road connects with anything.

Derek puts his damp hand on my shoulder. "The reason the welcome center isn't open is because it doesn't exist yet. And the reason it doesn't exist yet, is because the BRIDGE ISN'T FINISHED YET!"

This is CA-RAAAAZY.

"Arcade?" Celeste groans. "I can't pry Doug's fingers off this cable."

"Hey, Doug?" I say gently, trying to take his mind off the horrors of our predicament.

"Yeah, friend. I'm h-h-ere. N-n-n-ot going anywhere."

"Oh, good. Well, I was reading a library book about this place. The Golden Gate Bridge . . ."

"Yeah. C-c-c-california. H-h-how come it's so c-c-cold in C-c-california?"

"Well, we're right at the Golden Strait, on the windy, foggy coast. That's why they call it the Golden Gate Bridge, you know. Heh-heh. Has nothing to do with the color."

"Y-yeah. C-c-cool."

"And since we're here while they're still building the bridge, it's important for you to know that they've installed a safety net right below us. I read about that. So, no worries, right, friend?"

I look over at Doug's stiff frame, grasping the steel. He relaxes for an instant, and Celeste succeeds in prying his fingers off the cable.

"Shake your hands out, bud," she says, "before they cramp."

Doug shakes and takes a deep breath in, then out.

Okay, token. We've seen California. You can take us home now.

"ARCADE LIVINGSTON! GIVE ME THE TOKEN!"

A man emerges from the fog on one side of the ramp. A Badger brother.

Which one are you?

I hold my hands out. "I DON'T HAVE IT! I PUT IT IN THE COIN SLOT!" I hold up the empty chain, and it flashes a light beam in his direction, knocking him off his feet.

"THE TOKEN IS MINE!" The other Badger brother emerges from the fog, passing the one still on his back on the ground. "It will return, Arcade. And then, you *will* HAND IT OVER TO ME."

Zoe grabs my hood from behind. "Run, Arcade! I have your back!"

"Yeah! We GOT YOU!" Derek and Celeste jump between me and the Badgers.

I turn and run. Knowing there is no way *over* this bridge.

Feet stomp behind me and my friends scream, "GO ARCADE! GET OUTTA HERE! WE'LL KEEP THEM BACK."

A fog bank blows in, covering the path in front of me.

How much longer can I run? And then what?

My glasses fog over again, and I wipe them with my sleeve.

Lord, I need help! Show me a way out of here! Show me a way over this bridge!

And then the cloud moves, and sunlight once again clears the view. It's an amazing sight. Blue sky, blue water, brown hills . . .

I just wish there was a gray road ahead. But there is that net . . .

I look up and spy a cable that isn't attached to the road

yet. I'm coming to the last few steps before the road ends. I turn my head and see all my friends running just a few steps behind me. Behind my friends, another cloud has moved in. I can't see the Badger brothers anywhere.

"Derek!" I yell, closing in on the end. "We're going to jump, grab that cable, and drop into the net."

"NO!" Everyone yells at once.

"Okay, then, any other ideas?"

And right then, an electric shock flows through my body. It feels like getting hit by lightning—well, maybe. Zoe points to my chest, where the Triple T Token has landed back on the chain.

"Let's get outta here!" She holds out her hands to catch the fog, which has turned into glitter.

Huge elevator doors, in international orange, rise at the end of the roadway.

Much better than swinging from a suspension cable!

Now the coin slot rises up right at the end of the road too. I pull the token off the chain . . . and someone grabs it from my hand!

"I TOLD YOU, IT'S MINE!"

This Badger brother tilts his head back and lets out an evil laugh. It's the same laugh I hear sometimes when I go through the doors.

"NO, IT'S MINE!" The other brother tackles him right on the edge of the roadway. One wrong move and both of them will tumble off the bridge. With the token.

"YOU DON'T DESERVE IT! YOU WERE NEVER SUPPOSED TO HAVE IT!"

"YES . . . I . . . WAS!"

It's a full-on wrestling match now. The doors are fading, and the coin slot is blinking like it's going to short out.

And then I remember what the old lady at the library told me, weeks ago, when she first put the chain with the Triple T Token around my neck:

"You're name's Arcade? Then this is for you."

Yes. It is for me. My name's on the back!

My heart pumps, and I clench my fists. I step forward, take a deep breath, and jump right into the middle of the wrestling match.

"Arcade, DON'T!" Zoe reaches forward to grab me.

But she doesn't have to join the fight, because the token jumps right back into my hand!

"HEY! GIVE THAT BACK!" One of the brothers stands and tries to take the token. The other jumps up and pushes him toward the edge. He falls, grabs his brother's leg, and they both tumble out of sight and into the fog!

"OH, NO!" Jacey covers her mouth.

I can't see a thing through my wet glasses, except the pulsing coin slot, blinking even more now and beginning to fade away.

"I need to put the token in before it's too late!" I throw the token in. Then I put my palms together and pull them apart. The doors open, but the entrance to the elevator is a short leap out from the roadway.

Oh. No.

"Come on, Dougie! You can do this!" Celeste grabs Doug's hand.

Lord, help him over!

Doug closes his eyes and leaps, and we all follow him into the huge, foggy elevator.

"To truly live, you must forgive." A woman's voice echoes throughout the elevator. I look around for her, but I can't see a thing. "Oh, how I wish they'd forgive . . ."

We landed back on Derek's bridge at Forest Games and Golf. It was just like all the other times through the doors—no time had passed. The crowd, now unfrozen, watched as Jacey took a picture of me on the bridge.

"Last plank! Last plank! Last plank!" the crowd was chanting and encouraging Derek.

They were waiting for Derek to secure that last plank so that the bridge would be complete. Derek looked over at me and whispered, "Do you see them anywhere?"

I turned in every direction. No sign of the Badgers.

I shook my head and bent down to talk to Derek. "They fell off the bridge, I think. I couldn't see with the fog so thick. They may be hanging in a safety net in about the year 1935. I don't really know how all this works."

Derek quickly secured the cables to the plank, sweat streaming down the side of his face. "Well, I'm glad we're almost finished, so we can get outta here."

I glanced over to where Zoe, Doug, Celeste, and Jacey

were standing, right at the edge of the bridge, looking a little shell-shocked.

"Arcade, smile!" Jacey held up her phone and clicked a picture.

"That can't get out to anyone, remember? Anonymous!"

"I know," she said with a wink. "I just want it to remember this awesome week."

Ten minutes later, Derek stood and put both hands up in a victory pose.

"DONE! Who wants to walk over the new Forest Games and Golf bridge?"

People lined up. I stepped aside. I was kinda done with bridges for now. I walked over to the pole which now served as the bridge tower so I could take a picture of the golden plaque:

Forgiveness

And clue three came to mind:

To truly live, you must forgive.

Forgiveness must be a tough bridge to cross with someone.

I wonder what the Badger brothers need to forgive each other for?

"Hey, Arcade! You wanna turn on the waterfall?" Jackson came running over.

"What waterfall?"

"Come on and check it out!" Jackson led me and the group over to a rocky area right behind hole eighteen.

"Every creek needs a water source. And now that the creek isn't blocked by the windmill, we can let the river flow! Go ahead! Flip the switch and see if this baby still works!"

Jackson took me over to one of the rocks near the wall. Another golden plaque was there with a red button next to it. The plaque said *Restoration*. Below it, just like the others, were the words, *Arcade Adventures*.

"Do I push *this* button?"

"You see any others?" Zoe laughed and poked me in the ribs.

I pushed it. The pipes rumbled and squeaked. We waited.

"Maybe the pump is broken, or the pipes are rusted out," Derek said. "Maybe I can take a quick loo—"

But then the water let loose. It shot in all directions at first, like a broken sprinkler head. We all squealed as it soaked us. But then the flow smoothed, and streams of water cascaded down over the rocks. It was a beautiful waterfall, feeding a flow of clean water into the creek that ran under the bridge, next to the village house, behind the windmill, and back to the pump where it would send it back down the waterfall again.

Jacey gasped. "We did it, Arcade." But her smile quickly faded. "Do you think the Badger brothers will ever see it?"

"Not until they're ready."

CHAPTER 36

Breaking the News

Jaden delivered us to Derek's house at 3:30 am, just minutes before Aunt Weeda returned from her job taking inventory. None of us had time to jump into bed, so we faked being asleep on the couch. All except Loopy, who was so glad to see all of us that he jumped from body to body, licking and barking.

"Loopy! Those kids are sleepin'!" Aunt Weeda came over and kissed all of us on the forehead one by one. Zoe stretched and pretended to wake up.

"I sure hope you all had a more relaxin' night than I had! Woweee. I'm glad to be home. And guess what? I have tomorrow off! I'm thinkin' it's time to celebrate with some chicken pot pie and cake from the Bridgeview Bakery."

"That sounds great, Aunt Weeda." Zoe yawned.

"And, I have a little surprise for you and Arcade too." She grinned like a rascal.

"A surprise?" I said out loud without thinking. "I don't know if I can take too many more surprises."

She pointed at me, grinning again. "I thought you were

sleeping! As for the surprise, you'll have to wait until the morning."

The next morning around nine, Zoe and I snuck out to visit Miss Gertrude.

"I hope she's here." We yawned and waited on the steps for five minutes. Just as we were about to give up, Miss Gertrude opened her screen door. She was still wearing her robe and slippers.

"Zoe and Arcade Livingston! I am so glad to see you two. Get on in here!"

She had a zip in her step that I hadn't seen the last time we were here. She led us into the living room. Goldie jumped into my lap the minute I sat down on the pink, flowery couch.

"So, tell me, how does the windmill course look?"

Don't you want to know what happened to the brothers?

"It's beautiful, Miss Gertrude." Zoe beamed. "The windmill is back up, the structures all have fresh paint, the bridge is rebuilt, and did you know there's a waterfall? We turned it on last night!"

Gertrude rocked in her chair, her hands clasped over her chest. "Restored to how it was before?"

I shrugged. "I guess. We never saw it before."

"And did those awful Badger brothers get in your way?"

"They tried, but then they disappeared."

"Do you know where they went?"

I shook my head. How could I even begin to explain?

Gertrude addressed Goldie, "Didn't I tell you that Arcade Livingston had a good heart?" Goldie just meowed.

Miss Gertrude got up from her rocker and began to escort us to the door.

Getting rid of us? So soon? We have so much to talk about. The brothers . . . the token . . .

"Would you like me to keep an eye on the house, and let you know if they come back?"

Zoe nodded. "That would be helpful, thanks. The project is done, but I don't think we're done with them yet."

That reminded me of something. "Miss Gertrude, why didn't you tell us there were two Badger brothers?"

She stared at me through the closed screen. "Didn't you read my note on the paint card? On the back?" She shut the door.

The paint card? Pattie's Paints?

It was in my back pocket. It pays not to change clothes sometimes. I pulled it out and scanned it carefully. On the front was all the information about Pattie and the note from Miss Gertrude about her friend being willing to donate the paint. I turned it over. There was *another* note I hadn't seen! It was also in Miss Gertrude's handwriting:

Yes, Mr. B has a brother. They're twins! And they're my grandsons.

CHAPTER 37
The Big Surprise

y midmorning, we were all napping on the couch. Too many late nights. Aunt Weeda was a ball of energy, though.

"You kids are gettin' lazy this summer. I need to find you more work to do! Come on, minivan leaves in twenty minutes!"

Doug, Derek, and I moaned and groaned. Every one of my muscles was sore. My head was sore. Even my teeth were sore. Probably from gritting them for the last few weeks.

Zoe and Celeste didn't seem much better. They both threw on sunglasses and ball caps before they met us out in the van. Zoe still had a streak of yellow paint on her forearm.

"Where're we goin', Mom?" Derek rode shotgun and appeared to be the only one keeping track of our route. The rest of us tried to snooze in the back.

"You'll see. We're about to add a couple of people to our summer party!"

Anybody but the Badger brothers.

We drove for a while, and eventually turned into the place where this whole summer "party" started. Lynchburg's airport. Aunt Weeda parked the car and checked her watch. "Their flight should be landin' in five minutes." She turned to look at us, all half asleep in the back. "Come on! You young people can carry the luggage."

We trudged through the parking lot and entered through the door that led to a baggage carousel. We plopped down on the rocking chairs that were scattered in the lobby.

"What? Get up! These people deserve a peppy greeting!" Aunt Weeda put her palms out and raised her hands up and down. "Get up, now, come on! Their flight has arrived."

"DOTTIE! ABRAM!" Aunt Weeda ran toward them with her usual snack bags in hand.

"Mom! Dad! What a surprise!" Zoe ran and hugged them. "Are you here for a vacation?"

Mom grinned. "A short one. It wasn't really a good time for it, but your dad convinced me. The house was way too quiet without you and Arcade."

Dad came over and gripped me by the shoulder, smiling. "I think you've grown since I last saw you. But how can that be? It's hardly been two weeks."

I stood up a little straighter, and Doug answered for me. "He's been eatin' a LOT of cinnamon bread." Then he slapped me on the back.

"Someone get these bags off the belt," Weeda said as she moved toward the exit. "And we'll go get some of those famous baked goods on the way home."

"We can only stay for a week," Mom said. "You kids can fly back when we originally planned."

Dad grinned. "And we arranged our schedules so that we have a little more time to spend with you in New York before school starts again."

My stomach jumped a little at the thought of starting *another* new school. Junior high this time.

"So, what do y'all want to do while you're here?" Weeda smiled back at our big group that was smashed together on the bench seats in the back of the van.

Dad closed his eyes and tipped his head back. "Relax!"

"You know what I'd like to do one day?" Mom peered out the side window. "I'd like to go play at Forest Games and Golf. I haven't been there in ages." She turned to me and Zoe. "Do you know that's where your dad and I used to hang out when we were dating?"

Aunt Weeda pulled the van into the parking lot at the Bridgeview Bakery. "Mmm-mmm! I can smell good things from here! Let's go in and eat, shall we?"

We all piled out.

I hope Jacey is working. She has to be tired after putting in so many long nights this week, though.

"ARCADE! Yay! You're here." She *was* working. "Wow, what a huge group! Did you come for lunch?"

"Yes, we did," Aunt Weeda said. "Miss Jacey, I'd like to introduce my brother and his wife. This is Dottie and Abram."

Jacey came around to the front of the counter. "So you're Arcade's parents? It's so nice to meet you."

Zoe whispered in my ear, "Well, they're *my* parents too."

I put a finger to my lips to shush her.

Jacey looked around the busy bakery. "Would you mind sitting outside? I can set up some more chairs and a big table and pull over an extra shade umbrella for you."

"That would be delightful, honey." Aunt Weeda pushed

me and Derek forward. "And take all these children with you to help. The adults will stay in here and order the food."

Jacey grinned. "Okay." She turned to the guy behind the counter. "Victor, make sure you give them the family discount, okay? And throw in an extra loaf of cinnamon bread." She looked over at me, and her eyelashes fluttered. That girl needs to get some safety glasses to keep all the flour and sugar out, I guess.

"Follow me." Jacey led us to a back room off the kitchen that had a bunch of plastic chairs stacked up inside. "Have you guys seen the news this morning?"

You had time to watch the news?

"Everyone is talking about the restoration of Forest Games and Golf! The parking lot was packed first thing this morning. People couldn't wait to play the windmill course!"

"Oh, dear," Zoe said. "I hope all the employees can keep our secret."

"I'm sure they will." Jacey pulled some plastic chairs off a stack and handed them out one by one.

"The news reporter said that the owners, Lenwood and Kenwood Badger, were unavailable for comment." Jacey sat down on one of the chairs. "Where do you think they are, Arcade?"

"I'm thinking San Francisco. Mid 1930s."

"But do you think they'll be back?"

I shrugged. "I guess only this little golden travel guide knows for sure."

I reached down

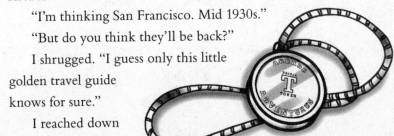

to touch the Triple T Token, and the crazy thing heated up! "Really? Now?"

You find out the why after you go.

"Arcade, what did you *do*?" Zoe just doesn't get how I'm still not in control of this.

"Are you guys in for another Arcade adventure?"

"Are you kiddin'? I'm totally in!" Derek stepped next to me, just as the glitter began to fall. The doors appeared, and the coin slot flashed just as brilliantly as it always had.

"This thing *could* be taking us back to the Golden Gate Bridge, you know."

"I don't care, I'm *all in*!" Celeste adjusted her cap and stepped toward the door. "This is the best summer ever! I got your back, Dougie!"

"Okay, then, if you're *sure*." I reached up for the token and it came off the chain and fell into my hand. I took a deep breath. "Here we goooooo!" As I threw it in the slot, I made the open-door motion with my hands. The elevator dinged, and Jacey, Celeste, Derek, Zoe—and even Dougie—followed me in.

B EFORE or AFTER?"

My annoying voice again. Blaring over the elevator speaker.

"Arcade," Zoe put both her hands on my shoulders and glared into my eyes, "do you care about me at all?"

"Huh? That's a ridiculous question, and I'm the king of questions!"

She narrowed her eyes. "YES or NO?"

"Of course I care! You're my only sister. My opposite." I glanced over and grinned at Doug.

Zoe sighed. "Oh, good. Then would you please, please, PLEASE, pick one of the *actual* choices? Puh-leeeeeeaseeeee? For me? Just this once?"

"Just this once?"

What could I do? She'd been suffering from my out-of-the-box choices ever since we started this crazy trip to Virginia. It couldn't hurt to choose something on the menu for once. Just. This. Once.

The choice wasn't hard this time. I've always been

interested in the origins of things. Beginnings are exciting. So I walked up to the one red button, held out my palm, and proclaimed my choice.

"BEFORE."

There is some *serious* water spraying all around us! We're wearing blue rain ponchos, and the hoods are pulled up over our heads. Tons of people are standing around, and they're squealing. I pull my glasses off my face so I can see. We're on a huge boat.

"Dude!" Doug yells. "I know where we are! Niagara Falls!" He gurgles the word 'Falls' as a splash of water hits him in the mouth.

"So we're back in New York?" Zoe wipes the water from her eyes and pulls her hood further down over her forehead.

"Well, we *could* be in Canada," I say. Zoe pushes me over.

"What? I'm not kidding! I read a book about this. Niagara Falls is on the border of New York and Canada. We could be navigating Canadian waters right now."

"I'd like to think I'm in New York," Jacey says, and she pulls her hood off, letting the waterfall spray drench her hair. "I've *always* wanted to go to New York."

Okay, so we're in New York.

The squealing and drenching continues for a few more minutes, and then the tour boat rides out of the waterfall's spray. We reach a point where we can look out and see the awesome power of the water that is pouring over the Niagara Falls.

"Now *that's* a waterfall." Celeste crosses her arms. "Not like that silly old one at Forest Games and Golf."

"It's breathtaking." Zoe actually pulls her hood off so she can look up.

We all hang over the railing and take in the amazing sight. Never have I seen so much water flowing freely, anywhere. People all over the boat are taking pictures. I try to do the same, but as usual, my phone shows nothing but glitter whenever we are on an adventure.

Zoe speaks again. "I think the waterfall at the Forest Games and Golf has its own special kind of beauty. Miss Gertrude was practically in tears when we told her it was working again. What was it she said to us, Arcade?"

I have to think a minute. And as I do, my back pocket heats up. I reach back and pull out the golden envelope. The one with the three clues in it. I open the envelope and count the clues. One, two, three.

Still only three.

But . . . wait . . . there is one more scrap of paper crunched down at the bottom of the envelope. I step away from the boat railing and sit on one of the empty benches behind all the tourists.

"What is it, Arcade?" Jacey comes and sits right next to me. Zoe joins me on the other side.

"There's a clue number four!" I unfold the tiny paper that has a small golden four printed on the front.

I have to squint to read it, even with my glasses.

> ## Hole number eighteen: Restore to what it was before.

Zoe peeks over my shoulder. "Hole eighteen? The one with the steel netting?"

I shake my head. "I don't think so. I think it means *all* the holes. Remember what the plaque on the waterfall said?"

"Restoration!" Jacey proclaims.

"That's exactly what Miss Gertrude asked us about the golf course! Remember? She said, 'Is it restored to what it was before?'" Zoe popped up on her feet. "I think the whole windmill course represents a life journey."

"One that requires humility, generosity, and forgiveness?" Jacey smiles.

"Yes. And that leads to *restoration*." I fold up the clue and put it back in the golden envelope. "No wonder the course fell apart. Somewhere along the line, the brothers lost their way."

"Hey, what are you all doin' back there? Planning snacks for the cruise home?" Doug waves us back to the railing.

"Nah," I reach down for my chain, and the golden travel guide has returned. "But I think I know of a way for the Badger brothers to make it back home."

As soon as I say that, Niagara Falls turns to glitter.

Discussion Questions

1. The first T on the Triple T Token stands for . . . TRAVEL! Had you already figured that out? How did you come to that conclusion?

2. Do you like to travel? Why or why not? What has been your favorite place to travel to? Why? Where is one place you would NOT like to travel to? Why not?

3. Imagine you are Arcade Livingston (*That's dope!*). You've just inserted your Triple T Token into the golden coin slot, stepped through the elevator doors, and after a bumpy ride, you've arrived in that place you *never* wanted to go (see your answer to question 2)! What will you do next?

4. The old woman on top of the pyramid tells Arcade that he learns the "why" after he goes. Have you ever said to someone "*Why* do I have to go?" or "*Why* am I here?" Did you learn the reasons why?

5. Find a globe (you probably have one in your classroom). Close your eyes, spin it, and then stop it with your finger. Is your finger pointing to a piece of land? If not, try again until it does. Then Google that place or go to the library and find some books about that place. Write a list of five interesting facts about the place. Tell about whether or not you'd like to travel there and why or why not.

6. Every time Arcade enters the elevator doors, he has one button to push. But is he actually given a choice? Do you think Arcade is controlling the process at all? Why or why not?

7. Do you ever feel like you don't have control over where you go or what you are doing in your life? If so, what are some things you *do* have control over?

8. After a few trips through the elevator doors, Arcade is convinced that he's supposed to help Mr. Badger fix up his mini golf course. Did you think this would be a difficult task for Arcade? Why or why not? What do you think would be harder for Arcade—fixing the course or ignoring the feeling that he's supposed to fix it?

9. What was your favorite Arcade adventure from this book? The trip to Arcade Adventures where his parents first won the token? The pyramids? Holland, India, the hospital on Arcade's birthday, the Golden Gate Bridge, or Niagara Falls? Why was it your favorite?

10. The windmill course represents a successful life journey—one that requires humility, generosity, and

forgiveness. What is humility? Why do you think humility is necessary for success?

11. How have people shown you generosity? How did it make you feel? How can you be generous to the people around you? Give generosity a try this week and see what happens!

12. Where do you think the Badger brothers ended up at the end of the book? Do you think it's too late for them to forgive each other? Is it ever too late to forgive someone?

13. Miss Gertrude cried when she found out that the windmill course had been restored. Is there anything in your life that you would like to see restored (made new again)? Is there anything you can do to help that happen?

14. Now you know what one of the three Ts stands for! Do you have any guesses about the other two Ts? Write your guesses here: _____

_____

15. Tell a friend about Arcade's adventures! Share your favorite parts of the story and which character is your favorite. Now challenge your friend to read the books and see if he or she can guess what the three Ts stand for.

Acknowledgments

First and foremost, thanks to you, my Lord and Savior, for allowing me to become not only an author but a best-selling author! I also thank you, God, that in a very short time I am now also known as a children's book author! You never ever cease to amaze me!

Momma and Daddy Jennings—you continue to play a role in every waking moment of my life. If you hadn't brought me into this world and taught me in your own ways that nothing is impossible with faith and hard work, I would not be in such a privileged position today—and writing these Arcade books. I love you!

Jill Osborne—We're rolling! I can't say enough about how impressed I am with your pure writing talent and your ability to help make what I envision for the Arcade series a reality. We brainstorm. We pray. We laugh. We write. And by God's grace, we win! I knew I'd picked the perfect writer to partner with on a project that is so near and dear to me. You help me to perfectly capture my message of love for kids! Thank you!

Keith Bell—Your creativity and commitment to all things Arcade Livingston continue to remind me of why God caused our paths to cross. I know you'd rather play in the background, but I want to put you on blast for a moment to say how much I appreciate you for all you're doing with this series. You help make Arcade live! And you and I both know that we're just getting started!

The Zondervan/Zonderkidz Team—I truly appreciate the opportunity your company is giving me to bring Arcade to the world! I sense a very long and prosperous authorial relationship brewing. I never thought I'd write one book, let alone multiple books. Let's keep the conversation going and growing!

And to every kid who reads this book—Know that I see you. I believe in you. You are amazing. And if you're not already enjoying your own Arcade adventures, stick around. My buddy Arcade is sure to inspire you to get started. Keep your eyes out for the next book. And as always, enjoy the ride!

Read the excerpt from

ARCADE
AND THE FIERY METAL TESTER

book 3 in the

COIN SLOT CHRONICLES SERIES!

rcade, QUIT pushing the elevator buttons! You *don't* have control over them."

"CHILL, Zoe! I think by now I know what I'm doing."

"No, you DON'T. This is the *Empire State Building,* not one of your arcade token adventures."

I stepped back from the button panel and wrapped my hand around the Triple T Token that was hanging from the gold chain around my neck. It had been in my possession almost six months now—heating up and pulsing whenever it felt like it, taking my friends and me on journeys around the world, into my past, and even into my future! Today, the token kept its cool, hanging there like any medallion would do. *That* was a relief. I stared at the display above the elevator doors.

78, 79, 80 . . .

My older sister, Zoe, and I were on our way up to the top of the Empire State Building to meet our parents. They had left a note for us on the dining room table that hot, August morning:

> *Zoe and Arcade,*
> *Meet us at 1:00 pm on top of the Empire*
> *State Building. Tickets are in the attached*
> *envelope. We will have our annual back-to-*
> *school goals talk there!*
>
> *Love, Mom and Dad*

And now it was 12:45. Dad always says that on time is *late*, so our only option was to be early. Especially since we were going to have the dreaded *goals talk*.

"This is a pretty smooth elevator ride." Zoe bit her pinkie nail while she drummed her fingers on her bent elbow.

"You nervous?"

"Me?" Zoe pointed her thumb at her chest. "Why should I be nervous?"

"Goals . . . back to school . . . talks with parents . . ."

Ding!

The elevator doors opened. We stepped out and were greeted by a smiling lady whose badge said her name was Marjorie.

"Welcome to the 86th floor."

I grinned. "Thanks! But doesn't this building have 102 floors? I'm pretty sure I read that in a fifty-pound coffee table book I checked out from the library."

Her eyes brightened. "*New York City: A Coffee Table Tour?*"

"Yeah, that's the one!" I pointed my index finger toward the sky.

Zoe rolled her eyes.

Marjorie continued, "I have that book at home. It's a favorite. And you're *quite right*, young man. There are 102 floors. What's your name?"

"Arcade Livingston." I held my hand out to shake hers. "Nice to meet you, ma'am."

"Arcade? What a magical name! Follow me, you two. The building narrows here, so you have to change to an elevator in the center to make it all the way to the top."

"So it's just like the subway, huh? I love it! Lead the way."

"Yeah, *just* like it." Zoe laughed. "Except we're *above* ground. *And* there are fewer people. *And* we're traveling vertically, not horizontally. Other than that, and a handful of other differences, it's *just* like the subway." Zoe cut in front of me, jostling me into the wall of the narrow hallway.

"What I *meant was*, it's like the subway because we have to *change cars*. When are you gonna start thinkin' like me so we don't keep having all these arguments?"

Zoe stopped and turned, crossing her arms. "Umm, never?!? And I prefer to call them *debates*."

"Of course you do."

Marjorie led us to a special elevator in the middle of the building. "Here you go, young people. Enjoy the rest of your ride. It's a beautiful day. You'll be able to see forever. And make sure you come back and check out the 86th floor open-air observation deck."

"We'll do that on the way down. Thank you, ma'am." I stepped into the elevator car and Zoe followed. The doors closed.

Ding!

I reached for Triple T. It was cool to the touch, just like it had been ever since the middle of June when Zoe and I returned from our cousins Celeste and Derek's house in Forest, Virginia. Cool was perfect. It had been the hottest summer ever recorded in New York City, and I needed some time to figure things out.

The display above the doors clicked away. *100, 101, 102 . . .*

I opened my mouth and tried to yawn. "Are your ears plugged?"

"Huh?" Zoe pressed her finger in front of her ear and wiggled it.

Ding!

"WHOA! That was the quickest elevator ride of my life!" I stepped forward. The doors opened, and this time a smiling gentleman apparently named Reynold greeted us.

"Welcome to the top of the Empire State Building! You're in luck, you're the only ones up here. That hardly ever happens."

"Really?" I stepped out of the elevator to have a look around. "This is dope!"

Zoe chewed away on her nail. "Are you sure there's not a married couple up here? Our parents are supposed to meet us at one o'clock."

Reynold shook his head. "Haven't seen 'em yet. And I see *everyone* who makes it up here to the top."

"Hmmm. I wonder if we should wait here for them." Zoe looked around and took her pink and purple tie-dyed backpack off her shoulders.

Reynold led us toward the enclosed, circular observatory. "Not necessary. Go ahead and enjoy the view. When they arrive, I'll let them know you're here."

"First one who finds the Times Square ball wins!" I yelled, and we both charged in opposite directions.

Zoe headed to the left side of the building, and I went right. No surprise there. I scanned the horizon filled with skyscrapers, water, ferries, and bridges below. I found the Statue of Liberty. It looked like the size of a chess piece!

"Whoa."

"There's the Brooklyn Bridge!" Zoe pointed out. I'd been over it in a taxi only once, but there was no mistaking it.

I wanted to keep staring out, but I had a game to win, and from all my study of the geography of Manhattan, I knew I was looking south. Times Square was north from here. I turned and made my way toward the other side of the building so I could beat my sister to the ball.

I raced alongside the windows, focused on the New York City skyline, but before I reached the north end of the observatory, I ran right into a little old woman wearing white sweats and a . . . Triple T ball cap! My mouth hung open. I had seen her only a few times before. And the first time I would never forget. It was at the Ivy Park library right after our move to New York City. The day she gave me the Triple T Token and wished me, "Happy travels."

She sat there, knocked to the ground, her ball cap glowing with gold and silver glitter. "Arcade, you're getting big."

I reached out a hand to help her up. "I'm so sorry! I didn't see you there."

She stood, brushed herself off, and stared at me.

I looked around. Reynold was nowhere in sight. "How'd you get up here?"

"Elevator," she said, raising an eyebrow. "Just like the subway."

I laughed. "I like how you think."

"I like how *you* think. That's why you have the token."

"Yeeeeaaaahhhhh. About that. I have a LOT of questions for you, like—"

She put her hand on my chest. "Sorry, no time. But I do have to tell you one thing. Things are about to heat up. In all areas. To test your mettle."

My metal?

"It's all part of the process."

Process?

"Trust the tester . . ."

Tester?

"Arcade!" Zoe's voice echoed in the distance. "I found the ball! I win!" I turned to see Zoe standing by a window in the corner of the observation room. She had her phone out, taking pictures, no doubt to record the moment and have proof that she won.

"No! I hate losing to my sister!"

When I turned back toward the old woman, she was gone.

The Coin Slot Chronicles
Arcade and the Triple T Token

New York Times Bestselling Author Rashad Jennings

The Coin Slot Chronicles series, by former NFL running back and *Dancing with the Stars* champion Rashad Jennings, is a humorous and imaginative series that explores the power of friendship and imagination, the challenges in finding your place, and the reality of missing home.

Eleven-year-old Arcade Livingston has a problem. Several, actually. The Tolley twins, a.k.a. neighborhood bullies, are making Arcade's move to a new city even harder than it needs to be. They expect him to do their research papers and interactive displays for the sixth-grade career expo's theme: "What do you want to be when you grow up?" Besides doing their work, Arcade doesn't even know his own answer to that question.

Then at the library—Arcade's favorite place to chill—a mysterious old woman gives him a golden arcade token that grants him a unique gift. A gift that allows him to time travel between different places including his own future. From sitting in the dugout with Babe Ruth, to hanging on to the back of a bucking bull, to performing life-saving surgery on a dog, Arcade has no shortage of adventure! Together with his older sister, Zoe, Arcade explores life's biggest thrills and challenges, and the two also have a big mystery to solve. Who is the rightful owner of the incredible Triple T Token that leads to such astounding adventures?

Arcade's circle of friends begins to widen as the Triple T Token hangs from his neck. Pulsing. Beckoning another adventure. The question for Arcade, Zoe, and their new friends is no longer, "What do you want to be when you grow up?" It's "Where will we go next?"

- Great for reluctant readers
- Black and white illustrations included

Available in stores and online!

The Coin Slot Chronicles
Arcade and the Golden Travel Guide

New York Times Bestselling Author Rashad Jennings

Arcade and the Golden Travel Guide is the second book in the humorous and imaginative Coin Slot Chronicles series by *New York Times* bestselling author, former NFL running back, and *Dancing with the Stars* champion Rashad Jennings.

In *Arcade and the Golden Travel Guide*, Arcade, Zoe, and their friend, Doug, travel from New York to Virginia to stay with cousins and best friends, Derek and Celeste. It's a chance for Arcade to feel "normal" again after all the thrilling adventures in *Arcade and the Triple T Token*, book one in The Coin Slot Chronicles series.

But nothing is normal as long as the Triple T Token is hanging around his neck. Plus, Derek claims he's stumbled upon some troubling information, and now a suspicious person is following him. Arcade wonders if the trouble is related to the token—after all, someone has already tried to take it from him once.

Where did this Triple T Token come from? And are all the adventures it provides worth all the trouble it brings?

As Arcade, Zoe, and their friends start to put the pieces together, the value of the token becomes clear, and the stakes are higher than ever. Can Arcade keep the token for himself? Or will sinister forces steal it from his grasp?

- Great for reluctant readers
- Black and white illustrations included

Available in stores and online!

The Coin Slot Chronicles
Arcade and the Fiery Metal Tester

New York Times Bestselling Author Rashad Jennings

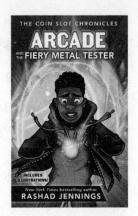

In *Arcade and the Fiery Metal Tester*, New York City is experiencing the hottest summer on record. Eleven-year-old Arcade Livingston can't keep his cool after receiving this suspicious warning atop the Empire State Building: "Things will heat up in all areas to test your mettle."

In no time flat, Arcade is tested like never before to use the Triple T Token's powerful ways to outsmart a bully, find a place for his best friend to live, and spy on some pesky villains. Meanwhile, his sister Zoe thinks controlling the token is nothing but a path to disaster.

One thing's for sure, the token continues its flashing and pulsing. And elevator doors continue to transport Arcade, Zoe, and their friends to meet different people in strange locations—people who will challenge them, teach them, and inspire them to grow in patience and compassion.

And just as a trip through a fiery furnace is necessary to purify gold, the token leads Arcade through superheated situations to test the purity of his heart.

Read as part of the series or as a stand-alone novel! *Arcade and the Fiery Metal Tester* is the third book in the humorous and imaginative Coin Slot Chronicles series by *New York Times* bestselling author, former NFL running back, and *Dancing with the Stars* champion Rashad Jennings.

- Great for reluctant readers
- Black and white illustrations included

COMING February 2020!

IF in Life

*How to Get Off Life's Sidelines
and Become Your Best Self*

**New York Times bestselling author
Rashad Jennings**

In his debut book, *The IF in Life: How to
Get Off Life's Sidelines and Become Your
Best Self*, former NFL running back and *Dancing with the Stars*
champion Rashad Jennings shares his inspiring story and experiences that will encourage readers to follow their dreams.

As a kid, Rashad was overweight, had poor vision, asthma, and a 0.6 GPA yet he still hoped to one day play in the NFL. The odds were stacked against him, but through hard work and determination, Rashad became a record-setting running back who has played with the Jacksonville Jaguars, the Oakland Raiders, and the New York Giants.

In *The IF in Life*, Rashad writes about the decisions that shaped his life. From overcoming injuries and setbacks to reaching goals and everything in between, Rashad's transparency about his journey will encourage readers to hold on to faith in the midst of uncertainty and win big in life.

Perfect for anyone looking for an inspiring story, this book also features photos from Rashad's childhood, college years, and professional career. Bonus poster included in the hardcover.

Available in stores and online!